the one that
got away

Carol Rosenfeld

Bywater Books
Ann Arbor

Bywater Books

Copyright © 2015 Carol Rosenfeld

Bywater Books First Edition: June 2015

Printed in the United States of America
on acid-free paper.

Cover designer: TreeHouse Studio

Bywater Books
PO Box 3671
Ann Arbor MI 48106-3671
www.bywaterbooks.com

ISBN: 978-1-61294-060-1

Earlier versions of Chapters 14 and 18 appear in "Q&A,"
a short story published in Best Lesbian Erotica 1999,
edited by Chrystos and Tristan Taormino,
published by Cleis Press, Berkeley, California

This novel is a work of fiction.
All characters and events described by the author
are fictitious. No resemblance to real persons, dead
or alive, is intended.

To those who love me, even when I'm bad

Acknowledgments

The journey from inspiration to actual book took approximately twenty years. The manuscript went through numerous workshops and readers as well as a title change.

I am grateful to:

Maureen Brady, who read the first twenty-five pages nearly twenty years ago and told me the book would be published someday. Maureen's constructive criticism and unflagging support helped the manuscript to grow;

Toni Amato, for reading and commenting on it; I regret that the U.S. Postal Service lost the package;

Greg Herren, who wanted to publish it but didn't get the chance, through no fault of his own;

Paul Willis, for reading and commenting on it;

Don Weise and Julia Pastore, for reading and commenting on it;

Guillermo Filice-Castro, a wonderful poet and

photographer, for helping me with Eduardo's Spanish;

Thomas Keith, for reading it, commenting on it, recommending it, and taking a proprietary interest in it—I could not have asked for a more supportive advocate;

Michele Karlsberg, who took the manuscript under her wing, and flew forward with it in her inimitable style;

Jess Wells, who picked up where everyone else left off, and helped me to get to the final manuscript; and

Trent Duffy, always my rock in the stormy seas of my life.

And to my family, friends and colleagues who have cheered me on, scheduled me for readings, attended my readings, critiqued pages from the book in workshops, and shared my excitement—your happiness for me has been the best part of the publishing experience.

To my dear friend, Pris DeLong—I should have sent you the manuscript when you asked me to, but I wanted it to be perfect, so I waited. I thought we had time. I'm sorry you never got to read this, because you wanted to.

Finally, to Kelly Smith, Marianne K. Martin, Salem West (with special thanks for getting me through the last 5%), Ann McMan, and Marlo at Bywater Books—I feel blessed that you have taken me on.

the one that
got away

"When you fish for love,
bait with your heart, not your brain."
Mark Twain

"Many men go fishing all their lives
without knowing that it is not fish
they are after."
Henry David Thoreau

"Nothing makes a fish bigger than
almost being caught."
Author Unknown

Prologue

In the days before the Internet enabled us to stalk people, memory was our primary link with ex-friends and lovers. A capricious power, memory remains drowsy until roused by some seemingly random thing or event— a song, a diary entry, a ticket stub, a restaurant. But memory can't answer the question that sometimes tags along on the journey: what if?

My therapist once said that when you're climbing a mountain, sometimes it's good to pause and look back at how far you've come.

It's a beautiful fall day today, not unlike the day of an encounter with a woman who blazed through my world like Halley's Comet. Her name was Bridget. Bridget McKnight.

Chapter 1

"We want the best," William said.

"Of course." Eduardo's tone implied that surely this was why they had chosen him to plan their wedding.

It was an ordinary morning, if such a thing exists in the bridal industry. An early October morning with lingering humidity, the last guest to leave summer's party. My boss, Eduardo, and I were having a power breakfast with two new clients, William Meany III and Patricia Blank. They were both investment bankers.

As I held out the basket of no-fat bran mini-muffins to the bride-to-be, she smiled and sipped her black decaffeinated coffee. "I'm trying to lose some weight before the wedding."

Sighing, I wondered where, oh where, was the woman who would declare, "I want to grow into my wedding gown," and demand muffins worthy of the name, with butter and jam.

I am well suited to be a bridal consultant, having muddy hair and a full-moon face. My legs are short enough for the shortest inseam, while my waist and hips require a trip to the women's department. It's a body that is neither good enough nor bad enough to be noticeable, making me an inoffensive handmaiden for those who are primping and preparing for their brief blaze of glory.

"Could we do the ceremony at St. Patrick's Cathedral?" William asked.

"You're Catholic?"

"Well, no. Does it matter?"

"It could be a problem. Religions tend to be a bit territorial."

"We'd be happy to make a contribution," William said. "We need a place that's big."

"What kind of numbers are we talking about?" Eduardo asked. "Just a rough estimate for now."

"Say, four hundred, four hundred fifty."

"I'd love to have that orchestra that played in Central Park for the reception," Patricia said.

Eduardo said, "I believe the New York Philharmonic has a rather busy schedule."

The only son of a well-to-do Argentinean landowner, Eduardo arrived in New York and found his first patrons among acquaintances who remembered the spectacular Buenos Aires weddings he'd helped to arrange for his sister and cousins. His dream client was an Astor or a Rockefeller, though his current customers were people who wanted to flaunt their money, or people who wanted to create the illusion that they had more money than they really did.

Eduardo wore his long, silky raven hair in a tightly plaited ponytail. He clothed his flapper's body entirely in black, flowing through the world like ink from a calligrapher's pen. His solemn demeanor was aided by round, wire-rimmed glasses he didn't really need.

According to Eduardo, his mission in life was to bring elegance, glamour, and drama into a lackluster world. He liked to say, "Many are called, but only ten percent are chosen."

Eduardo also liked to say, "These women tell me, 'I've been waiting my whole life for my wedding day.' But really, what is one day? I can feel special anytime. I just put on a gown and party."

—*mm*—

On the way to our next meeting, I popped into Dunkin' Donuts. To me, a proper power breakfast is one packed with sugar.

"What is that?" Eduardo asked.

"The Manager's Special." Draped in thick chocolate icing and extravagantly garnished with rainbow sprinkles, it oozed some sort of gloppy substance that I was hoping might turn out to taste of lemon. Or apple.

Eduardo shuddered.

We were scheduled to meet Nancy McKnight, our second client of the day, and look at bridal gowns. At the previous session, Nancy had tried on practically every gown in the shop without choosing anything. "They're all so beautiful," she'd said.

The evolution from engagement to wedded bliss can defeat even the strongest-willed woman. I have watched confident, independent women certain of wanting something simple and practical, find themselves several months and one mother later dragging a twelve-foot train down the aisle.

But Nancy McKnight was spineless from the start—incapable of making a decision about anything.

We took a cab down to Orange Blossom Thyme on Spring Street. Shopping for a gown was one of the more difficult tasks in the wedding planning process for Eduardo. He'd confided to me that he always wanted to try on a gown himself, and occasionally found himself thinking he'd look better than the bride in some of them.

Nancy was already there, and Gloria Hewett, the shop owner, was showing her some new gowns that had arrived the day before.

A woman walked into the shop, carrying a container of coffee. And in one perfect *Miracle Worker* moment I understood desire the way Helen Keller understood the word "water."

"This is my sister, Bridget," Nancy said, heading for the dressing room.

I stood there, willing her to take my hand.

Instead, she said, "Hi."

A trapdoor opened in the plateau of my life and my heart fell through, flattening into a red carpet at Bridget's feet.

"It's good that you're here," I said. "I think your sister needs some help in choosing her bridal gown."

Nancy came out in a gown.

"This brings back memories of Halloween, Nance," Bridget said.

"Did Nancy dress up as a bride one Halloween?" I asked.

"Every Halloween," Bridget replied. "She didn't trick anyone."

"So what?" Nancy said. She smiled at herself in the mirror.

"I had to escort you, that's what. No matter what I wore, everyone knew it was me because I was with you."

As Nancy returned to the dressing room, I asked Bridget, "What did you dress as?"

"A pirate. An ice hockey player—I blacked out some of my teeth for that one. The Abominable Snowman. The Cowardly Lion—I loved that costume. I wore it to bed and played with my tail all night."

When Nancy came out in her second gown, Bridget said, "That one looks nice." She said the same thing

16

about the third and fourth gowns. The latter was one of the most unflattering bridal gowns I had ever seen on any client. Bridget winked at me. I blushed. She smiled then. It seemed to come from deep down inside her, spreading across her face like the sun coming fully up and over the horizon. None of the women I'd made love with in dreams and fantasies had ever had a face. Not until Bridget smiled at me.

Nancy called out from the dressing room, "The zipper's stuck."

I went in to assist her.

"You have a great job," Bridget said, as I put the fifth gown back on its hanger.

"I do?"

"You get to see women in their underwear."

We regarded each other in comfortable silence for a long, drawn-out moment. Then I said, "Actually, the highlight of my day is when the Federal Express woman delivers."

I opened the file with Nancy's personalized calendar and checklist. "Y'know, we should be looking for a dress for you, Bridget, since you're going to be Nancy's maid of honor."

"Why don't we talk about that over a beer?" Bridget said.

"OK." I pulled out my daily planner. "When?"

"She's free every night of the week," Eduardo said. He was fingering the pleated organza train on a Caroline Herrera gown.

Bridget laughed. "Why don't we meet Thursday night at Naked Promise?"

"That's a bar, B.D.," Eduardo said. "A lesbian bar."

"You've never been to Naked Promise?"

"No," I said, "but it's on my list of things I need to do."

"Bring that list with you on Thursday night. I'd like to see it. Maybe I can help you."

17

That Thursday night, Bridget stood, beer bottle in hand, scanning the room, checking out the women, who were checking her out. As far as I was concerned, she was the only woman in the room worth looking at.

Bridget wasn't that much taller than I. She was big in the way that women sculpted by Maillol are big—with assertive hips and a grounded stance. When she stood behind me, I thought of those Russian dolls that nest inside one another. And then I thought of a line from a song that goes, "The bigger they come, the harder they fall." I can't explain exactly what it means to me, but it's something good.

One of the things I notice about people is their hair. Bridget's hair had weight and mass. It wasn't very long, but there was a lot of it; the colors of autumn. I imagined it cloaking my hands, curling around my fingers, tickling my palms.

"Nancy had a screwed-up childhood," Bridget explained. "Our mom was always telling her one thing, while our dad was telling her something else, so eventually she just gave up and let whatever happened happen."

I understood that. After all, I had sat on a fence for years, watching my friends and relatives, gay and straight, date and mate, while I held back from entering the fray myself.

"But what about you?" I asked Bridget.

"I never listened to either of them," she said.

My feet were starting to hurt. I tried shifting my weight as I sipped my beer.

Bridget was like the sister I sometimes wished for. As an only child, the most adventurous thing I'd dared to do during my time spent under the parental microscope was to contemplate making a rope from my sheets and climbing out my window. I never did, of course. A sister like Bridget would have provided continual diversions, and I might have been able to slip off and sneak a cigarette or spray some graffiti.

Bridget confided to me that she hadn't worn a dress since she'd left home at seventeen.

"Don't you have to get dressed up to go to work?" I asked. "What do you do?"

"I'm a motivational speaker. I go around to business conferences and make speeches about how you can have more fun at work and be more productive."

"How did you end up doing that?"

"I know about teamwork, about motivation and self-discipline," Bridget said. "I'm a jock." I listened as she talked about the joys of basketball, biathlon, canoeing, ice hockey, parasailing, racquetball, tennis, and wrestling. "I have a conference in Lake Placid this winter, and I think I might be able to try luge." I envisioned her in one of those shiny skintight bodysuits the Olympic lugers and speed skaters wear.

"Is there any place to sit down in here?" I asked.

Fortunately, there was an empty stool at the bar. Bridget eyed my half-full bottle before ordering another beer for herself. "You're a cheap date," she remarked.

"I'm easy too," I replied. Bridget laughed. People never take me seriously when I want them to.

"Eduardo always introduces me as, 'My assistant, Miss B.D.,'" I said. "Most people hear it as Bea Dee, and call me Bea or Miss Dee."

"Is Bea short for Beatrice?" Bridget asked.

"Actually, B is just the letter. My initials are B.D."

"So what does B.D. stand for?"

I sighed. She was going to have to be told at some point. I took a swig of Rolling Rock, squared my shoulders, looked her straight in the eye, and said, loudly and clearly, "My name is Bambi. Bambi Devine."

The bartender snickered.

"It's a good thing you're not a butch," Bridget said.

I leaned forward, bending down slightly, tugging the hem of my skirt to cover the lace from my slip. I wondered if Bridget was watching, and hoped it wasn't too dark in the bar for her to notice my cleavage. When I looked up at her, she was smiling at me. A flush started in my toes and raced up to the roots of my hair.

"How did you get your job?" Bridget asked.

"I met Eduardo at a conference sponsored by the alumnae association of my art school. He was ready to hire an assistant, and I was bored with what I was doing at the time."

"Where did you go to art school?"

"At the only all-woman art school in the country."

"That must have been fun."

"Actually," I said, "I wasn't out to myself then, so I didn't really benefit from the situation."

"So when did you come out?"

"About a year ago, I guess."

"Did you sleep with men?"

I nodded.

"And?"

"At best, it was like making do with McDonald's when what I really wanted was a leisurely dinner at a four-star restaurant."

"And at its worst?" Bridget asked.

"I'd rather not talk about that," I said. I could feel the dark waters of the past beginning to swirl.

"Drink up," Bridget said gently. "I want to see you finish that beer before we leave."

The next day Eduardo and I discussed the problems presented by Nancy's wedding while taste-testing the creations of an up and coming catering firm.

"Well, we can't put Bridget in a typical maid of honor dress," I said. "It would be . . . sacrilege."

"You mean for the dress?"

"No, for her. She has a kind of muscular lushness."

"You mean she's hot, *dulce*. That's what you're trying to say, right? And I can tell you a hot butch like that has no business in a gown." Eduardo sighed. "I don't know what I'm going to do with this bridal party. The bride can't make up her mind about anything, and the ring bearer asked me if he could be the flower girl instead.

"In this business, people resist the exotic," he continued. "No spicy food because grandma can't take it. Most of our clients think that serving quiche instead of those wretched miniature hot dogs is daring."

I had a fondness for miniature hot dogs. At least you could tell what they were.

"Eduardo," I said. "What are we eating?"

"Caribbean ratatouille blinis."

I decided I was going to stop off at Gray's Papaya for a hot dog on my way home.

"I've been thinking we should offer a support group for butch women who have to be bridesmaids and wear dresses," I said.

Eduardo rolled his eyes. "B.D., I know you'd love to be the only femme in a room with a bunch of butch women, but do you really think they're going to share their feelings about having to wear a dress? Please, honey. A butch support group is when they all get together and rebuild an engine or something."

I pictured Bridget in a white t-shirt and faded blue jeans, a greasy rag hanging out of her back pocket, bending under the open hood of a car, wrench in hand. Then I tried to visualize her in the maid of honor dress Nancy was considering—a buttercup yellow crepe sheath with a matching bolero jacket swirled with gold beads. Eduardo hated the dress; he claimed it was proof the designer was a misogynist. Still, it was easier to imagine Eduardo in the dress than Bridget.

Chapter 2

If you're going to come out later in life, New York City is a good place to do it. It has an LGBT bookstore, Ozmosis, and an LGBT community center. Not to mention Greenwich Village.

My time with Bridget at Naked Promise had been an interesting experience, but I needed a different kind of knowledge. So the following Saturday I went in search of the one source of information I could always count on—books.

Yet standing outside of Ozmosis, I was reluctant to enter. I was thinking about how sometimes a group of animals can sense a stranger, and refuse to accept one of their breed because it doesn't smell right. I took a couple of deep breaths. I was a lesbian. Ozmosis was an LGBT bookstore—it said so right on the door. And, in all probability, the customers and staff were LGBT. So what was my problem? Maybe I was too old.

I pushed the door and entered, dropping my shoulders, relaxing my jaw, trying to look and act as if I'd been in the store hundreds of times.

"Check your bag, please."

At least that felt familiar.

I handed over my sturdy canvas tote, worn and smudged by city soot. The clerk handled it a little gingerly. Maybe I should look for a new tote bag in the store I thought.

Standing by New Releases, I could see a section labeled Lesbian Erotica. There was a woman standing in front of the rack, reading. I took up a position at the Humor section directly across the aisle and studied her while pretending to look at a book on the history of lesbian hairstyles. She was wearing a black leather jacket and button-fly jeans. Her bright red hair was shaved close to her head. There was a small silver hoop through her left eyebrow, and two large rings on her right hand. She was reading Fisting with Finesse.

She looked up and over at me. "Did you squeak?"

"I didn't say anything."

"Not speak, squeak." Her voice seemed very loud. "I heard a squeak."

"Must have been the floor." I twisted the soles of my Easy Spirit pumps back and forth on the wooden boards. "Excuse me," I said, moving over to Mystery.

There I found another woman in a leather jacket, looking down at a small open notebook in her left hand. She was a bit shorter and much thinner than me, and her dark hair was boyishly cut. A man in the Travel section seemed to be watching her. He took a few steps toward her, squinted, then turned away.

I pulled a book off the rack and began reading the description on the back cover.

"That one's good, but her most recent one's even better," the woman said.

"I like to read mystery series in order," I told her. "Do you know what the first book in this series is?"

"I don't remember, but I can check it for you. I just have to go into a different file. This is the list of books I want to read. I have another list of books I've read. And

24

I also have a list of mystery series in chronological order. My name's Ellen."

"B.D.."

While Ellen was opening the file, I looked at her some more. I liked what I saw. She was obviously well organized, and we both liked to read mysteries. I wondered if it was too soon to suggest having a cup of coffee. I'd noticed several tables and a pastry case in front near the display window.

"I have to hand it to Sue Grafton," Ellen said. "You can figure out the order of her series by the titles alone." She meant the author whose titles create a crime-themed primer: *A is for Alibi, B is for Burglar, C is for Corpse,* and so on.

"The covers of the Brother Cadfael series usually give a number," I said.

"I've never read any of those," Ellen said. "Who's the author?"

"Ellis Peters. The detective is a medieval monk."

"I'm not religious."

"Neither am I, but sometimes I think I was a nun in a former life," I said.

Just then a woman came up behind Ellen and put her arms around Ellen's waist—and an end to my idea of coffee.

"Honey, you can't buy any more books until you get rid of some of the ones you already have. It's in our contract."

"Just one, please?"

The new arrival turned to me. "I can't say no to my honey." She held out her hand. "I'm Annalise."

"B.D. I don't suppose you could recommend a couple of books for—a friend of mine who's new to all this?"

"For a baby dyke?" Annalise asked.

I felt the unmistakable heat of a blush.

"You're embarrassing B.D.," Ellen said.

"Why? You know I'm a magnet for baby dykes—you were one, once. Isn't that what the B.D. stands for?" Annalise giggled, and winked at me. "Should we tell her about the damn book?"

"*The Dam Book*?" I had heard of dental dams. Could there possibly be an entire book about them?

Ellen laughed. "We call it 'the damn book' because it's caused a lot of arguments among our friends. The real title is *The Persistent Desire: A Femme-Butch Reader*."

I followed them over to the Anthology section. Ellen frowned. "It's not here."

"Maybe it's in Sexuality," Annalise said.

"But it's an anthology," Ellen protested.

"Oh, please. Not everyone is as organized as you are, Pumpkin Toes." She looked at her watch. "Hey, we'd better get going if we're going to be at my mother's on time."

"B.D., give me your phone number," Ellen said. "Maybe we can all meet for coffee or something."

I watched as she entered my number into a device she was holding in her hand.

"This is an iPhone," Ellen said. "One day everyone will have one."

"My honey loves her toys," Annalise said.

"Lisey!"

"What? I'm talking about that thing in your hand, not the stuff in the box at home."

I saw that no one was in the Lesbian Erotica section, so I went over there. I stood in front of the shelf and decided to take just a quick peek at *Fisting with Finesse*. I jumped when Annalise, who had come up behind me said, "No, B.D., that's Lesbian Sex 102. You need Lesbian Sex 101. Try this." She pulled a book off the shelf and handed it to me—*What Lesbians Do in Bed (and Other Places): Step-by-Step Techniques Anyone Can Emulate*.

In the time-honored tradition of hiding the one thing you are really embarrassed about buying, I began piling up other books as I moved methodically along the shelves, selecting something from every section except Gay Male Erotica and Addiction/Recovery.

I chose *The Lesbian Quiz Book* from the Self-Help shelf. I had always enjoyed the quizzes in women's magazines. I liked filling in surveys too. I opened the book to the table of contents.

"What Kind of Women Are You Really
Looking For?
What Kind of Woman Is Looking for You?
Rate Your PC Savvy.
Top or Bottom?
Sex: How Do You Measure Up?"

I turned to "Weigh In on the Butch-Femme Scale":

1. To find a Phillips screwdriver, you would go to:
a) A hardware store.
b) A man named Phillip.

2. If you had to buy a chemise, you would look for it in:
a) An antique furniture shop.
b) A lingerie boutique.

In Sociology an index card bearing a staff recommendation was taped to the shelf beneath *Unseen Yet Omnipresent: Queer Infiltration of Popular Culture* by Maxine Huff. "Huff is HOT!" had been added to the bottom of the card in bright pink Magic Marker. I looked at the author's portrait. The woman in the black and white photograph made me think of a pixie with PMS.

A fringe of dark hair framed furrowed brows, and the thin seam of her lips suggested impatience with the photographer. I had an urge to press my thighs close together. I added the book to my stack.

Near the front of the store, a man sat behind a display case. He eyed my stack of books, arched an exquisitely shaped eyebrow, and said, "Maxing out your credit card?" A sign propped up on top of the glass read, "Nellie's Tchotchkes: Fill Your House with Pride Stuff." There were rainbow candles, rainbow flags, rainbow wind socks, rainbow pot holders, and rainbow switch-plate covers. If there's a pot of gold at the end of every rainbow, Nellie was sitting pretty.

"Are you Nellie?" I asked.

"In a manner of speaking," he replied. "I couldn't help noticing that you spent a great deal of time in the Coming Out section. Might I suggest one of our Starter Kits? The basic kit comes with a rainbow bandana, complete with styling suggestions, your choice of freedom ring necklace or labrys, a rainbow pen with purple ink, and this lovely journal." The journal had a photograph of Glenda the Good Witch on the front, with the words *Come out, come out wherever you are.*

"If you buy these items separately," he continued, "they would cost $65, but the kit is only $44.95. Our deluxe kit for lesbians has packages of lavender latex gloves, finger cots, and dental dams, plus six lube samples. So much less embarrassing than buying them alone, and only $12 more." He looked at me expectantly.

"I'll take the deluxe kit," I said. "And a pair of those ruby slipper earrings."

—ιμι—

When I got home, I pulled out the bandana and styling suggestions and put on the labrys and earrings. If I wore the bandana around my neck, it covered the labrys. If I wore it on my head I looked like I was getting ready for spring cleaning. Well, in a way I was.

"Look," I said to my cat, brandishing the labrys between two fingers. "The weapon of the Amazons." Truffle blinked at me. "Let's dance," I said, scooping him off the dresser and draping him over my shoulder.

"Y.M.C.A.," I sang, then hummed the rest, because I couldn't think of the words. Sliding sideways, I whirled around in a dancing fool's polka until Truffle stopped purring and started squirming. Then I put him back on the dresser, and he lay down under the lamp and began to clean himself.

"Now for the good stuff," I said, picking up *What Lesbians Do in Bed (and Other Places)*. The phone rang. I knew it had to be Renee because of the awkward timing. Renee always called during the denouement of a murder mystery, when the pasta had one more minute to cook, or as I was about to step into a bath. An offer to call her back, or even a blunt statement like "Uh-oh, something's burning," wouldn't dam the flow of Renee's stream of consciousness. I sighed and picked up the receiver.

"Bambi? I was expecting your machine."

"Hi, Renee."

"I heard this really funny lesbian joke, so I had to call you."

Renee was one of my straight friends. Or, as she liked to say, bisexual, because of the one time she'd had a threesome with a man and a woman. She felt this gave her an edge over my other heterosexual friends. Renee was thrilled that I had come out as a lesbian. She called me constantly with suggestions of movies to see, books to read, places to visit, and to ask if I'd had sex with a woman yet.

"OK. Tell me," I said.

"Tell you what?"

"That really funny lesbian joke. You said you called me because you heard this really funny lesbian joke."

"I did but I just realized I've forgotten it. I was going to leave it on your machine, but I was so startled when I heard your voice that the joke went right out of my head."

"Well, if you remember it, you can call me back."

"I will. Goodbye, Bambi."

I didn't wear the earrings, the bandana or the labrys the following weekend when I went to visit my parents.

At six o'clock my father was sitting in the wing chair near the front door, waiting for my mother to finish getting dressed. I was halfway down the stairs when she called to me, "Bambi, could you come here for a minute?"

I walked into my parents' bedroom, expecting my mother to ask me to help her with a zipper or a necklace. Instead, she said, "There's something I want to ask you."

I figured either she wanted to know if I was having money problems or she wanted my opinion on how my father was doing.

"You're not gay, are you?" my mother asked me.

"Are you sure you want to discuss this right now?" I said, thinking of our dinner reservation.

"Just answer me, Bambi."

"Are you going to get upset?" I asked.

"No, I just want you to answer me."

"Well, actually I am. Gay." I used her word. Now was not the time for a discussion about terminology.

"Since when?" my mother asked.

"That's a very complicated question, Mom." I tried to picture a time line of my life, with a bright pink thumbtack marking the moment.

"Well, I'm not happy about it, but I'm not going to lose you over it." I thought this was probably a shrewd decision, since I was her only child.

She fussed with the bow at the neck of her floral print blouse. "Are you going to tell everyone?" she asked, turning from the mirror above the double bureau to face me.

"If anyone asks, I'm not going to lie," I said.

My mother sighed. "I just don't want to have to talk to anyone about it, that's all." She pulled at the hem of her skirt. "Go downstairs and keep your father company. I'll be right there."

As I walked back down the stairs, I heard the water running in the bathroom sink for a long time. I tried to figure out what had prompted the conversation I'd just had with my mother. I felt vaguely cheated. I'd expected that coming out to my parents would be something I'd agonize over and finally work up the nerve to do, but my mother had taken control. She had an unnerving way of knowing when something was going on in my life. Maybe God had told her. She was always saying that she talked to Him every night on my behalf.

My parents' friends were waiting for us at the Chinese restaurant. I didn't pay too much attention to either my food or their conversation. I thought about what my mother had said: "I just don't want to have to talk to anyone about it." Presumably that included the two couples we were dining with that night. One of the women had known my mother for sixty years; the other had known her for nearly fifty. Both of them had sent me cards for every birthday I'd ever celebrated, even after I moved out of my parents' house. I'd see them at parties

31

and funerals, played with their children during summers at the seashore. I kept looking at their faces, trying to imagine their reaction if my mother shared her news. Could the simple fact of my being a lesbian so alter the way they felt about me?

Back at my parents' house, I changed into my pajamas and robe, hoping that something good would be on Turner Classic Movies. But when I walked into the room where my father was sitting in the recliner, feet up, with the cat on his lap, my mother said, "Martin, Bambi has something she wants to tell you." My father looked at me expectantly. My mother looked at her hands.

For many years I'd suspected that my father had quite a lot he could say, but something held him back. I couldn't put a name to it, but I could feel it holding me back as well. And so we faced each other across a chasm of unspoken words.

"I'm a lesbian, Dad."

He nodded then said, "Well, just be careful."

I knew what "be careful" meant. His cousin had died of AIDS, although of course no one in the family would say that. I had a strip of three photographs of the two of them, taken in one of those booths you find in arcades—my father, a dark-haired adolescent, and his cousin, a fair-haired, angelic little boy. But I felt sad that the first association that came to my father's mind when I told him I was a lesbian was disease.

"There's something I don't understand," my mother said. "You had that crush on Jerry Greenblatt all through high school, remember?"

Of course I remembered. I had a special portrait gallery in my memory for people who'd rejected me. But I suddenly thought of Jerry Greenblatt's sister, Judy. We'd been friends, and she had actually been more attentive to me, more appreciative of me, than he had. I wondered where she was now and what she was doing.

—✺—

When I returned to my apartment there was a message from Ellen.

"Hi, B.D. We thought you might want to go with us to Lesbian Film Night at the community center. Give us a call."

I fed Truffle and changed his water, then dialed Ellen's number. We chatted briefly, and I said I'd like to go with them.

I could hear Annalise in the background. "Tell B.D. to go to the community center and find out what film is on the program."

"But Lisey, B.D. can get that from the community center's web site; she doesn't have to go there," Ellen said.

Over the clatter of pots and pans, I heard Annalise say, "I want her to go there. B.D. is a dyke-in-training. She needs to check out the community center. Tell her to ask about the dances too."

"Did you hear that?" Ellen asked me.

"Yes," I sighed.

—✺—

Entering Ozmosis had been a bit unnerving, but walking down the sidewalk to the community center's doorway was like running a gauntlet. Men and women leaned against the side of the building and clustered at the edge of the sidewalk, chatting in couples and groups, some smoking cigarettes. I wondered whether the women were looking at me, and if they were, what they were thinking.

In the lobby, people gathered around a small board propped up on the reception desk. A lanky young man with bleached hair and an inch of dark roots sat behind the desk. A short, older woman with a tangled coif pushed her way through the crowd, the hem of her raincoat skimming the floor. "Where is the meeting?" she asked.

"Which one?" the man replied.

"The meeting. There's supposed to be a meeting here," the woman said peevishly.

"There are several groups meeting here tonight. What is the name of your group?"

"I just want to know where the meeting is," the woman whined. She turned to me. "Do you know where the meeting is?"

"No, I don't. I'm sorry."

A younger woman in a tailored navy pantsuit approached the desk. "Excuse me, but what room is the adoption group in?"

"Which adoption group?" the man asked. "Lesbian Couples Committed to Each Other and Contemplating Adoption or Lesbians with Issues About Being Adopted?"

I noticed a bulletin board with lots of flyers. There was one for Lesbian Film Night. I dug around in my purse for paper and a pen to write down the information. A man with thick, curly black hair came and stood beside me. I looked up at him, and he offered his hand.

"Ahmed."

"B.D."

Ahmed showed me an index card with "Cook for hire" plus a phone number, and pointed to the bulletin board. "May I?"

I shrugged. "I guess so, if you can find a spare thumbtack."

Ahmed seemed puzzled, so I just nodded my head, and he smiled. I wondered where he was from, and if he knew just where he was.

As I began jotting down the details of an upcoming dance, Ahmed read some of the other messages on the board. He tapped me on the shoulder and ran his finger underneath the words Turkish massage. "What is this?"

I pretended to knead invisible shoulders with my hands, though for all I knew hands and shoulders might not be involved, as the masseuse gave only a pager number.

Ahmed nodded and smiled. "Coffee?" He pointed to me and then to himself.

I sighed. Here I was in the Lesbian, Gay, Bisexual, and Transgender Community Center, surrounded by lesbians, and the only expression of interest had come from a man. Somehow, I knew Annalise would not approve. And I wondered what it might mean in terms of my new life as a lesbian.

Chapter 3

By the end of October, we had managed to get Nancy to narrow her choices for a bridal gown down to eight, and we were all back at Orange Blossom Thyme so she could try them on again. Bridget had apparently decided to call in some heavy artillery, for she announced, "I asked Natalie to meet us here."

Nancy wavered between terror and reproach. "Oh, Bridget," she whimpered.

If there'd been any traffic in the shop when Natalie came through the door, she'd have drawn the attention of the drivers away from the car in front of them. From her honeyed head that had seemingly never had a bad hair minute to her thoroughbred ankles, Natalie exuded chic.

We were a ragtag and bobtail group, greeting her. Bridget wore her usual jeans, oxford shirt, and boat mocs. The shop owner, Gloria Hewitt, looked like Cinderella before her godmother arrived, and my magenta silk blouse had creases at the elbow and waist. Only Eduardo began to approach Natalie's elegance. He took one look at her suit and whispered, "Armani," as though he were offering up a prayer.

Natalie wasted little time on introductions before turning her attention to the gowns, arranged in a row like suspects in a police lineup. She gave each one the concentrated deliberation of a witness trying to identify the perpetrator. Eventually she pointed to Number Six and said, "Let me see that one on you." Nancy scurried into the dressing room.

Bridget and Natalie didn't kiss or touch, but suddenly I couldn't swallow or speak. I could, however, hear the little Topo Gigio in my head sweetly asking me why Bridget had never mentioned her girlfriend.

Of course, I'd experienced selective omission before. Once, a man I'd been dating ate the entire dinner I'd prepared for him before he got around to mentioning that he was getting married to the former girlfriend he'd just returned from visiting.

While all of us waited for Nancy to emerge from the dressing room, Natalie turned her attention to me. "That color looks good on you."

If I'd had any spunk I would have said, "I know. That's why I'm wearing it," but if the queen singles you out for a compliment, just say thank you.

—*m*—

Nancy left, having acquiesced to Bridal Gown Number Six, and I had the satisfaction of crossing an item off our checklist. Bridget and Natalie were scarcely out the door when Eduardo proclaimed, "When God was handing out fabulous bone structure, that one snuck back in line for second and third helpings. *¡Qué divinura!* She looks better without makeup than most of our clients after an hour and a half with a cosmetician."

"Don't you think they make an odd couple, Eduardo?" I asked.

"In what way?"

"Well, if they were dogs, Bridget would probably be a golden retriever. With a red bandana," I said. "And Natalie would be a champion show dog—maybe a saluki."

"But the saluki might be weary of the show circuit, secretly craving a bit of rough and tumble with a rambunctious retriever," Eduardo purred. "And what a thrill for the retriever—humping a high-class, beautiful bitch. I bet those two have great sex."

It seemed a bit unfair to me that Natalie should have great bone structure and great sex too. But God does play favorites.

Eduardo looked at me. "Even though you want nothing more than to go home and eat Cherry Garcia by candlelight while you listen to torch songs, that's all the more reason for you to go out. Brooding is for hens, B.D."

Eduardo knew me too well. I was already indexing Ben & Jerry's flavors, hearing "I Don't Stand a Ghost of a Chance with You." When I got a break I called my friend Erica. We'd gone to art school together. Although, as I'd told Bridget, I hadn't been out to myself back then, Erica had been. I wanted to hear what she thought about the situation. "Do you have any plans for tonight?" I asked.

"Nope. What do you have in mind?"

"I thought we could do a Scotch tasting."

"What?"

"Like a wine tasting, but with Scotch."

"Is this some sort of event planning thing?" Erica asked.

"No. I want to go to a bar and order different kinds of Scotch."

"I'd better go with you, if only to make sure you take a cab home. Although I'm sure the story will be interesting."

"What story?"

"The one you're going to tell me while you're sampling Scotch."

Erica had the placid air of a Renaissance Madonna. Even her fine, dark hair, spun from the velvety center of a black-eyed Susan, refused to succumb to static. Over the years, I'd come to appreciate the irony that lay below. I'd seen her through some dissolute days; she was more jaded than Mick Jagger.

In the bar I stared at the menu. "It's just names and years of aging," I said. "Can't they give little descriptions, like Starbucks?"

Erica ordered two different brands for us and asked, "So B.D., what has brought you to this state?"

"I've met the woman of my dreams, and she's turned out to be someone else's reality."

Erica nodded. "Not an uncommon problem. Is she monogamous?"

"I assume so."

"Never assume, B.D. Ask her."

"I can't!" I said.

"Why not?"

"She'll know I'm attracted to her."

"Why is that a problem?"

"Erica, you know that I have a lot of experience in these matters. A lot of experience. When someone finds out that I'm attracted to them, it's not exactly like the Prize Patrol has shown up at their door. It's more like they've gotten a gift they don't really want and they're trying to figure out how they can get rid of it."

"B.D., I think you need to buck up your self-esteem a little," Erica said. She sipped her drink. "Do you really want this woman to be your first? Don't answer right away—think about it. The first time with a new person can be unnerving for anyone, gay or straight, but you're facing a double whammy—it's not just your first time with a particular woman, but your first time with any

40

woman. Would you run the marathon as your first race? Think of this as an opportunity, B.D. While the woman of your dreams is hitched to her girlfriend, you can be out there getting your sexual sea legs. Then, if they break up and she's interested, you'll be ready. You could also meet someone who will make you forget about her."

It might have been the Scotch, but I thought that Erica had made some good points.

"And if she is interested in you, knowing that other women find you sexy may increase her interest."

Chapter 4

Nancy inquired about our special, custom-designed "trousseau tour," which was basically a lingerie shopping excursion with a light lunch or tea included, courtesy of our company. This was something I'd put together, as I knew practically every source for lingerie in town—Madison Avenue boutiques, department stores, Victoria's Secret, plus one or two places that could be counted on to offer the truly tacky outfit I usually advised clients to buy because, as I assured them, "When it comes to lingerie, most men have limited imagination and even less taste." No one ever challenged this statement.

In addition to outfitting Nancy for her wedding day and honeymoon, I hoped to persuade her to allow Bridget to wear a tuxedo instead of a dress.

Bridget declined to accompany us. "I've seen my sister in her underwear plenty of times." But she agreed to meet me for a movie after the tour—the restored version of *My Fair Lady* was playing.

—ɯɯ—

After Nancy acquired a beribboned peignoir set that was a bit too busy for my taste, and I earmarked a lace bra and brief in a very attractive lilac color for purchase at a later date, we settled down to tea in a cozy second-floor shop.

"What was it like growing up with Bridget as your sister?" I asked.

"Oh, Bridget was always making me do things," Nancy whined. "I had to do whatever she told me, or she wouldn't leave me alone until I did. She made me ride real horses and go to the Fun House."

"I never found the Fun House to be much fun," I admitted. "It was scary."

"She took the training wheels off my bike and hid them." Nancy pointed to a scar on her hand. "She used to take my Barbie and Midge dolls and put them in compromising positions." Though I wasn't a mental health professional, the expression on Nancy's face and the tone of her voice conveyed to me that this mattered.

"I bet she beat up all the kids at school who bugged you," I said.

"Yes, she did do that," Nancy conceded.

A woman approached our table and asked if we would like to have our tea leaves read.

"I'd better not," Nancy said. "You might see something bad."

I placed my empty cup face down on the saucer and turned it around three times, the way my great-aunt Rose, who'd read tea leaves at Coney Island, had taught me to. The woman returned the cup to its upright position, peered at it intently, and announced, "I see a man, a handsome man with dark hair."

"Is he wearing a dress?" I asked, thinking that it might be Eduardo.

The woman looked offended. "Madame Roushka does not see such things," she hissed, stalking off.

I dismissed her vision as limited. But it had brought me back to my second objective.

"Bridget would look great in a tuxedo," I said to Nancy. "It would be cutting-edge chic. And since she's your maid of honor, your bridesmaids can still wear dresses."

"If my maid of honor wears a tuxedo, will the best man have to wear a dress?" Nancy asked.

"Not unless he wants to," I replied.

"That's OK, then."

—⁓—

I gave Bridget the good news when I met her outside the movie theater.

"Cool," she said. Then she asked, "So what did Nancy end up buying?"

"I can't tell you that," I answered. "Client confidentiality."

As it turned out, Bridget and I both liked to sit toward the back and on the aisle. "What a relief," Bridget said, as we settled into our seats. "Natalie always insists upon sitting farther down and in the middle."

"How long have you and Natalie been together?" I asked.

"About three years," Bridget replied.

"How did you meet?"

"At Disney World, at a tax law conference. Natalie's a tax lawyer. Most of her clients are art collectors."

From what Bridget told me, it appeared that Natalie had treated the Ivy League as a sort of academic salad bar, picking up a B.A. in Art History at Yale, an M.B.A. at Wharton, and a J.D. at Columbia. But she went slumming at New York University School of Law for dessert—an L.L.M. in Taxation.

"Natalie took me to a client's Christmas party once,"

Bridget said. "It was the only party I've ever been to where there wasn't any beer. The apartment was on Fifth Avenue, with a view of Central Park. And the art was just incredible. I guess I must have looked sort of clueless, because this guy started telling me about the paintings. Natalie told me afterward that he was the head of the Painting Department at the Museum of Modern Art."

"I've never seen a painting by a really famous artist in someone's house," I said. "I can't imagine looking at a Georgia O'Keeffe while you're eating breakfast."

"I never even went to a museum before I moved to New York," Bridget said.

"Does Natalie get invited to a lot of art show openings and parties?" I asked. "It must be sort of a fringe benefit of your relationship."

"Actually, she rarely takes me along. That Christmas party was hosted by two older gay guys, real sweet-hearts—they've been together since they were in their twenties—and I guess Natalie thought I might be an asset. But she never takes me with her if she's expecting to see her straight clients or business associates."

"Do you live together?"

"No."

"You mean lesbians can be in a relationship without living together?"

"B.D., the thing about lesbians renting a U-Haul on the second date is an old joke. You shouldn't buy into stereotypes."

"But don't you think some stereotypes start with a little grain of truth?" I asked.

"Well, I've only lived with one of my girlfriends," Bridget said. "And we moved in together after we'd been going out for a year."

"I'm not sure I would want to move in with someone right away," I said. "I've got a rent-stabilized apartment.

Besides, if I was living with someone, I'd feel like I had to be nice all the time."

Bridget laughed. "Trust me, B.D., that wouldn't last long. I bet you'd get cranky pretty quickly."

"Maybe I would. I think it would get on my nerves if someone was always in my space."

"Natalie and I set aside one night a week as 'date night.'"

"That sounds like a good way of keeping romance alive," I said.

"Actually, date night is for Natalie and me to spend time with other people, not each other."

"Oh," I said, wondering exactly how this arrangement worked. Did they see friends or date other people? What if the other person was always the same person? Did a date include a good night kiss? Was I on a date with Bridget without knowing it?

Chapter 5

When I thought about it, I realized that my day to day life hadn't changed all that much since I'd come out. I went to work, and most nights I watched television or read a book. Before I fell asleep I'd fantasize about someone who was unavailable and uninterested in me. The only difference was that now I was fantasizing about a woman instead of a man.

One morning Eduardo announced that he had bought me two tickets to the All-Girl Gala, an annual fundraising event for a foundation dedicated to researching lesbian health issues.

It was advertised as an elegant evening of cocktails, dinner, dancing, and dessert, as well as the presentation of awards.

"Thank you, Eduardo" I said, "but I think the All-Girl Gala is for couples, and, as you know, I am still flying solo."

"B.D., I checked with Wendy over at The Petal Pusher—she's doing the flowers for the event. She assured me that there will be single women there. Why don't you ask your friend Erica to go with you? Maybe you'll each meet someone."

"As my mother would say, 'From your mouth to God's ears,'" I replied. "But even if I did meet someone, I can't dance."

I had a long, sad history when it came to dancing. It began with my great Aunt Rose reading my tea leaves and telling me she saw me as a ballerina, twirling round and round. I took ballet classes, but that didn't last very long. At summer camp I attempted modern jazz dance until the day my bunkmates, who'd been outside the studio watching me, told me how ridiculous I looked.

I loved watching old movies starring Fred Astaire and Ginger Rogers, or Ann Miller, or Gene Kelly. I'd imagine myself moving with the music, graceful and light on my feet. But every dance I went to, I sat on a folding chair.

In spite of that, I had recently, on my own initiative, gone to a dance at a lesbian bar. I'd picked up a post-card at the community center for something I'd read as *Inhibited Tuesdays*. I thought it sounded perfect for me. When I took a second look at it, I saw that it actually said *Uninhibited Tuesdays*. Of course, when I thought about it, an event specifically for inhibited people wasn't likely to be much fun. Despite the daunting prospect of a room full of uninhibited women, I went. The room was dark and the music was deafening—no words or melody, just the throb of a bass underneath something that sounded like an artillery range. I slunk out before I finished my drink.

"Do you know that Emily Dickinson poem, Eduardo—the one that goes, 'I'm Nobody! Who are you? Are you—Nobody—too?' When I go to these community events, everyone seems to be somebody except me. I'm a no-body."

"No, you are somebody, bebé; you're B.D. Besides, the

All-Girl Gala will be different. It will be elegant, and there will be food."

"Do you know who the caterer is?" I asked.

"Blissful Bites," Eduardo replied.

"I'll call Erica," I said.

—~~~—

As it turned out, Erica was delighted by the prospect of attending. "The tickets are really expensive; I've never been able to afford one. I know you never went to your prom, but don't expect a corsage from me, OK, B.D.?"

Immediately after our arrival, Erica and I headed for the bar. Both of us scanned the crowd as we waited in line. When I saw Bridget, I nudged Erica and said, "See that woman over there—reddish-brown hair, black jacket, white shirt, black pants? That's Bridget, the woman I told you about."

"I see her—there's a woman bringing her champagne. And now they're toasting each other."

"Yes," I said. "That's her. Although the woman who brought the champagne isn't her girlfriend."

"She's not? Then who is she?"

"I don't know," I said. We were almost at the bar.

"Do you know what you want?" Erica asked me, as I stared at Bridget and the mystery woman. "To drink, B.D.," Erica said.

"I think I'll have Scotch again," I said.

Erica sighed. "Two Glenmorangie with water, please," she said to the bartender.

As we left the bar, drinks in hand, I headed away from Bridget and the mystery woman, toward a waitress with a tray.

"Stuffed mushrooms?" the waitress inquired. Erica and I each took one, and the waitress turned toward two women on the other side of her. One woman was bald, and sporting studs and rings in every place that I could see, and, I suspected, some that I couldn't. Her well-shaped naked mahogany head offered a pleasing contrast to the pale curls of her companion, who reminded me of Jean Harlow. *Hell's Angels* had been on Turner Classic Movies the previous week.

"Oh look," said the blonde, who had an appropriately breathy manner of speaking, "there's Maxine Huff— she's being honored tonight."

At least I knew the name, even if I hadn't gotten around to reading her book yet.

"I took her course last semester," the bald woman said. Her voice was as smoky as the fifteen-year-old Laphroaig Single Malt Scotch I'd had the last time I was out with Erica. I took a sip of my drink; there was no comparison with the Laphroaig.

"Sexual Politics and Practices?"

"That's the one. God, Huff is hot when she scowls at you. I used to be late for class on purpose."

"When I was in her class, her lectures were incredible, but the final exam was a bitch," said the blonde.

"Don't remind me. Who's the lucky girl with her?"

"You mean the imperial blonde? She's not *with* Maxine, she's her *friend*."

"I see someone I know," Erica said to me. "Stay here; I'll be right back."

I looked around the room and saw Natalie; then I realized that she was standing next to Maxine Huff. Natalie had to be the imperial blonde they were talking about; no one else in the room had that royal quality.

Another waitress came by with chicken satay. I hoped the two women would eat quickly and continue their conversation.

The blonde swallowed the last bit of chicken, patted her lips with a cocktail napkin, and picked up where

52

she'd left off. "I used to see her in Maxine's office practically every day."

"And you're sure they're just friends?"

"What I'm sure of is that Maxine's friend goes with that pretty butch with the luscious hair—the one with the cutie clinging to her."

I looked for Bridget, and saw that the mystery woman had her arm around Bridget's waist.

"For a couple, they're awfully far apart."

"Maybe they need some space in their relationship." The blonde giggled. Her friend chuckled. I pondered what it all might mean. Perhaps tonight was one of those "date nights" Bridget had told me about?

Erica returned. "It looks like people are starting to go into dinner. Shall we?"

As we made our way toward the ballroom, Erica said, "Well, I think I understand your attraction to—"

I grabbed her wrist hard and looked around us.

"I had no intention of saying her name," Erica said. "As it happened, she looked at me as I walked by. She appears to be comfortable in her body and secure in her sexual prowess. I must say, that woman with her—the one you said is not her girlfriend—is particularly affectionate."

Our table was at the back of the room. We sat down and introduced ourselves to the older couple already seated. Thelma and Valerie were both on the board of an organization called Older Dykes Still Doing It. Thelma had been married for thirty years. When her husband died, she learned computer skills to support herself, and through the Internet connected with Valerie, the gym teacher she'd had a crush on in high school. She went to visit her, and they fell in love. They had just returned from an Olivia cruise. Thelma handed Erica and me invitations to the premiere of the eagerly anticipated documentary *Secret Lives of Spinster Aunts*.

Bridget, the mystery woman, and Natalie were sitting

with Maxine Huff at a table close to the stage. Their backs were facing me, so I had an excellent view of the mystery woman's arm draped across the back of Bridget's chair, and of Natalie leaning into Maxine Huff.

Two more women arrived at our table. It turned out that each had come to the event alone. As they took their seats, the waitress came by to take our orders. The entree choices were broiled salmon, chicken Kiev, or pasta with vodka sauce.

Erica ordered the salmon.

"What kind of pasta is it?" I asked. I preferred not to deal with long strands of noodles in public.

"Penne."

"I'll have the pasta," I said.

"Are you a vegetarian too?" the woman to my left asked.

"No, I'm just craving a little carbohydrate comfort. Could you pass the bread basket, please?"

"I was hoping there would be more single women here," my table companion said. "I haven't met any lesbians at my Hadassah meetings."

No one responded to this remark; everyone picked up their programs and began reading them. I turned to the page featuring Maxine Huff.

"Maxine Huff is a tenured professor at Sisters of the Apocalypse College. She is best known for her erudite yet accessible monograph *Tea for Two: An Extremely Critical Analysis of Co-Dependency in Lesbian Relationships*, published by Pink Slip Press. Maxine is also the author of two other books, *Unseen Yet Omnipresent: Queer Infiltration of Popular Culture* and *Lesbian Bed Death and Resurrection*, which will be published next spring."

Maxine was introduced while people were finishing their entrees. She spoke briefly, and returned to her table. The band began to play, and couples began moving toward the dance floor. I wished that I could just go home, but I knew Erica wouldn't let me leave. And actually, I didn't want to miss the dessert buffet.

A tall, slender woman with short, silvery hair walked up to Erica. "Would you like to dance?"

"I'd love to."

I turned my chair away from the table so I could watch. Bridget was dancing with the mystery woman, while Natalie danced with Maxine.

"You two looked pretty good out there," I said when Erica returned after the music had ended. "But isn't she a little old for you?"

"I don't care what her age is; I think she's hot," Erica said. "And she wants my phone number. Thanks for asking me to come to this with you, B.D.. Can I persuade you to shake your booty?"

I sighed and started to get up from my chair. At the first few notes I cried, "Oh God, it's a salsa," and sat back down.

"B.D., you should just have fun. Look at all those women—most of them don't know what they're doing but they're having a great time doing it."

"I can't," I said. Where was the damn dessert buffet when I needed it?

"Look at your friend Bridget and her—well, let's just call the woman her date," Erica said. "They aren't really doing a salsa, but they're really into it."

"People are watching them," I said.

"People are watching them because they're heating up the joint," Erica said.

I could see that Bridget was definitely working her hips. Natalie and Maxine sat out the salsa but returned to the dance floor for the next number.

Eventually the dessert buffet was set up. I was the first one to pick up a plate.

At the end of the evening, Erica and I followed the quartet out onto the sidewalk, keeping them in sight while maintaining a respectable distance. Natalie and Maxine hugged. Bridget's friend kissed her, and then Bridget and Natalie walked off together toward the East Side.

"What do you think?" I asked Erica.

She put her arm around me and hugged me. "I'm so proud of you, B.D.," she said. "You're barely out of the closet and you're already in the throes of a dyke drama. What do I think? I think those four are the only ones who know the real story, and they're not about to tell it to us. Want to come to a party with me tomorrow night? I just found out about it."

"Where?"

"At a loft down in Noho. It's a fund-raiser for a lesbian filmmaker. No dancing."

"OK."

"I'll meet you there," Erica said, handing me a card with the date, time, address, and phone number.

As I reached the landing of the stairs, I was disconcerted by the appearance of two women sitting on chairs outside the entrance to the loft. One sported boxer shorts, the other wore plain, cream silk tap pants. Both had on cowboy boots. They explained that they had recently returned from a vacation in the Southwest.

"You have to take your pants off before you can go into the party," the woman in the tap pants said.

I cursed Erica silently. Had she known about this? I wasn't wearing anything particularly seductive or festive or even flattering underneath my black jeans—just black Jockey-for-Her briefs.

"That's OK. I'm just teasing you." The woman laughed and waved me on. I blushed, embarrassed by my credulity.

I went in, grabbed a beer from the bathtub that had been filled with ice, and began looking for Erica. There was an impressive spread on the table to one side of the room—cheeses and salamis, tomatoes, olives, pickles, grapes, Italian bread, plus potato chips and pretzels. I looked at the bottle in my hand. With a bottle in one hand and a plate in the other, I wouldn't be able to eat anything. I decided to finish the beer. Out of nervousness, I hadn't eaten anything before leaving for the party, so I began to feel the effects of the alcohol fairly quickly. I watched enviously as a woman loaded a plate. She wore a sturdy, faded denim shirt under a black blazer, and black pants. Her cinnamon hair angled across her brow and was tucked behind her ears. Her glasses had thick, black frames that made me think of photographs I'd seen of the Hollywood costume designer Edith Head.

I have a bit of a thing for girls who wear glasses. I still remember the scene from Truffaut's *Bed and Board*, where Antoine is in bed with his wife, who is wearing glasses and reading a book. When she closes the book, takes off her glasses, and turns to kiss him, he puts the glasses back on her. I found that very sexy.

The woman turned away from the table, looked up, and caught me staring at her.

"Not enough hands. That's the problem with buffet style, isn't it?" she said.

"Yes. I'm almost done," I said, holding up my beer bottle.

She smiled. I noticed that her lips, which were bare of lipstick or gloss or any kind of artificial enhancement, were a beautiful rose color. I decided that if I could market it I would call it Roseate Dawn. I tried to think of something interesting to say.

"Do you know anything about lesbian trios?" I asked.

She didn't seem at all disconcerted, and her response was gratifying. "Actually, I was one third of a trio for a while. Why do you ask?"

"Well, I think that someone I know—I mean, there's this woman I sort of, I guess you could say I have a thing for her, and I saw her girlfriend with this other woman, and then I overheard a couple of women talking about the three of them."

The woman nodded, carefully eating a piece of bread topped with salami and cheese. "Trios are a lot of work," she said when she'd finished. "In fact, at the end of the first year I was exhausted. I liked one woman more than the other, and I spent a lot of time and energy trying not to show it. What's your name?"

"My friends call me B.D."

"Sylvia Murray. So tell me more about this trio of yours, B.D."

"This woman I have a thing for—I'll call her Heart's Desire . . ."

Sylvia nodded as she popped a grape into her mouth.

"Well, Heart's Desire is in a relationship with a really beautiful woman. And last night I was at the All-Girl Gala with a friend—"

"So was I!" Sylvia said.

"And during the cocktail hour I saw Heart's Desire with one woman while her girlfriend was with someone else. And then these two women beside me started talking about the woman who was with the girlfriend."

"What did they say?"

"Apparently both of them had taken a class with the woman who was with the girlfriend."

58

Sylvia nodded again. "Were they talking about Maxine Huff?"

I stared at her, wondering if she could have been eavesdropping too.

"Well, Max was one of the honorees last night. But she also makes quite an impression on her students," Sylvia said. She thought for a minute and then continued, "So, if one woman was Max, the other had to be that blonde that she's always hanging around with. Now, someone— I can't remember who, but someone—definitely told me who the blonde's real girlfriend is. That would be the third woman, right? Heart's Desire I think you said. Shit! It's not Bridget McKnight, is it?

I didn't have to reply; the look of dismay on my face was enough.

"You've got great taste, kiddo! I've been trying to get into Bridget's pants for years!"

"Look, Sylvia, I'd appreciate it if you wouldn't discuss this with anyone."

"Not to worry, B.D. I don't get around much these days; I'm semi-retired from the community scene." She looked at me almost tenderly. "How long have you been out?"

"Not long enough, I guess."

"Have you been to bed with a woman yet?"

"No." I blushed.

"So, do you want your first sexual experience with a woman to be with someone you know, or do you just want to do it and get it over with?"

"Actually," I said, "I've been thinking of paying someone to do it."

Sylvia looked startled. "Oh, I don't think that will be necessary."

Erica interrupted us. After Sylvia excused herself, Erica said, "B.D., do you realize how long you've been talking to that woman? Will you please circulate?"

※

In the days after the party, I found myself thinking about Sylvia's question about my first sexual experience with a woman. I wondered if she might have been making me an offer I'd inadvertently refused.

Eve, my therapist, said Sylvia's question was inappropriate. "She should never have asked you such a thing."

"Why not?" I said. "It sure beats, 'So what sign are you?'"

I asked Annalise and Ellen if they thought Sylvia might have been making a pass at me.

"You may look, act, and talk like a femme, B.D.," Annalise said, "but sometimes you think like a butch. A true femme would have snapped at that like a trout trying for a fly."

I was depressed at the thought that I might have closed a window of opportunity. Who knew when another one might open?

I found Sylvia's name in the phone book, wrote out a script for what I wanted to say, and practiced it before dialing the number at two o'clock in the afternoon on a weekday. Despite the probability that she would be at work, as I was, I was still relieved when her answering machine came on.

"Hi, Sylvia, this is B.D.. We met at that party last week. I was wondering if you might like to have dinner sometime." I left my home and work numbers and hung up.

Sylvia returned my call the next day. We arranged to meet at a Thai restaurant in Chelsea on Saturday evening.

※

Saturday afternoon as I poured bubble bath under the running water, I started to think about toothbrushes. What did you do if you were going out on a date and might not end up coming home until morning? I didn't want to carry a purse. The idea of using someone else's toothbrush was disgusting, although when I thought about it, that didn't really make sense, because when you kissed someone you were in contact with the same parts of their mouth that their toothbrush was.

Dinner was pleasant. The food was good and the conversation flowed fairly easily. We talked about books and music and Sylvia's job as a set designer. Afterward, we walked through Chelsea toward the Village.

"Y'know that question you asked me, at the party?" I said. "About my first sexual experience with a woman?"

"Uh-huh," Sylvia said.

"I don't suppose you meant—"

"No," Sylvia said. "But after the party I was afraid you might have taken it that way."

"Oh, I didn't," I said. "I was just wondering."

When we reached West 4th Street, Sylvia said, "I think I'm going to head back to Brooklyn. Take care of yourself, OK?"

On the way home I bought the Sunday New York Times and a pint of Häagen-Dazs German Chocolate Cake ice cream. After I closed the door behind me and locked the locks, I unzipped my jacket, took my toothbrush out of the inside pocket, and put it back on the bathroom sink.

Chapter 6

It seemed strange to be talking about a day in June when the sky was battleship gray and the air was an icy slap in the face.

"You do understand that we're not talking about the June of this coming year, but the next one," Eduardo said.

The bride-to-be sat in the chair placed at the corner of the coffee table diagonally across from me. Her fiancé, seated to my right, had disturbed the symmetry by moving his chair closer to hers. They were holding hands. Now he turned to her and said, "You mean we have to wait a year and a half to get married just so we can have the reception at some garden? Can't we do it somewhere else?"

I wanted to laugh at his naiveté.

"It's not some garden, David. It's the New York Botanical Garden," the woman said.

"Isn't that in the Bronx? Kelly, what about my mother? You know she doesn't travel west of Fifth Avenue or above 72nd Street."

"One word, David. Limo."

"Well, I don't know, Kelly."

I watched as Kelly's face began to take on the all too familiar look that preceded a major tantrum. But she had the presence of mind to shift into a simple pout for her beloved's benefit.

"Well," David began.

I kept watching Kelly. Now she looked like she was trying to work up a few tears. I might have underestimated her acting abilities.

"If it's what you really want, sweetheart." David's capitulation was complete.

It was easy, in the lethargy of late afternoon, to convince myself that antlers were growing from David's head, and transpose him into a trophy over a mantle. I thought the wedding ring should go through his nose instead of on his finger.

Then I glanced out the front window and witnessed the silent arrival of the first snow of the season, large flakes swirling around like cheap tissue confetti. I forced myself to focus on my notes, although I really wanted to run to the window and shout, "Look, it's snowing!" By the third or fourth snowfall I would be more blasé, but right now I was a child again.

Eduardo paused between sentences, and I knew he'd seen it too. I looked over at him and saw satisfaction in his expression. Things were proceeding according to plan.

Growing up in the Southern Hemisphere and celebrating Christmas in the summer had offended Eduardo's innate sense of propriety. It was a relief to him to finally be able to indulge in seasonal festivities at the appropriate temperature.

"Don't worry, David," Eduardo said as he escorted the happy couple to the door. "There will be plenty for you to do in the next year and a half. The time will just fly."

"Did you see those tears?" I asked Eduardo as we carried boxes of ornaments marked "Ofc" up from the basement. The boxes marked "apt" remained below for the tree-trimming portion of Eduardo's annual all-day holiday fête, held the Sunday before Christmas. "When the straight-to-DVD vampire film she's supposedly starring in is finished, you have to rent it and invite every gay man you know to watch it. And I want to be there to hear what they have to say."

Eduardo celebrated Christmas in a big way. No sooner had I finished digesting the stuffing from my cousin's Thanksgiving turkey than Eduardo began his annual holiday rituals.

"You're coming to my fête, aren't you B.D.?" he asked. "I'm starting with brunch again, served on the Spode Christmas Tree china, followed by *Miracle on 34th Street*. From 1:30 to 5 we'll trim the tree, and then we can watch *It's a Wonderful Life*. Dinner will be at 7."

"Served on the Wedgwood or the Royal Doulton?"

"I haven't decided. I know traditionally I've used my grandmother's Royal Doulton, and this dinner party is steeped in tradition, but I just got the Wedgwood and I'd like to show it off. And of course, we'll walk off all those calories with some caroling, then return for *White Christmas* and wassail."

"Oh, Eduardo," I said. "It will be all men, and I feel like I've reached a point in my evolution as a lesbian where gay men aren't going to be much help."

"You mean you're not going to meet someone at my fête who will go to bed with you," Eduardo said. "You're right about that, but you're also wrong because what you need to be doing right now is finding your family. We can't choose the family we spend the first part of our lives with, but we can create the family that we want to live our lives with. You know, B.D., I wanted Kris Kringle to be my father. I wanted to be an orphan like the little Dutch girl, sitting on Papa Noel's lap, while he sang to me in my native language. My father knew, B.D.; he knew very early on. I would try on my sister's hats or reach for one of her dolls and my father would say, 'Maricón,' and turn away. I was defective, an embarrassment, something to be ignored. You've become a member of my family, bebé, and it's important to me that you be part of my Christmas celebration."

"Then of course I'll be there, Eduardo," I said. "Though I may get a little depressed around the mistletoe."

"Stay near the cookie tray."

I perked up. "Is André coming?" André the baker had a pastry shop around the corner from our office. At last year's party he had brought an enormous tray of delicious, exquisitely decorated butter cookies.

"Yes, André told me he'll be there. B.D., go outside and let me know how our tree looks from the sidewalk."

I stood in front of the window, shivering, and nodded my head. Eduardo drew his eyebrows together, then arched them and smiled. There was a man standing next to me. He'd stopped to look at the tree. He had gray hair, a neatly trimmed beard, and sapphire blue eyes. He was tall enough and wide enough for me to hide behind if I wanted to.

The man laughed and I saw that Eduardo was using a ball ornament as a mirror and smoothing his hair into place. Eduardo heard the laughter, looked up, and winked. The stranger considered the tree, then pointed to the top right.

Eduardo indicated a bare branch with his finger and mouthed, *Here?*

The stranger nodded. Eduardo smiled, held up one

66

finger, disappeared, and returned carrying an ornament, a silver bear in a Santa suit. He carefully hung it from the bare branch and looked out, searching for approval. The stranger gave him two thumbs-up.

Eduardo held up one finger again. A minute later he was opening the door. "Would you like to see the tree from another perspective?" he asked.

There was a moment of silence, then the stranger said, "Sure, why not?"

Eduardo escorted the visitor into the front room. "My name is Eduardo, and this is B.D."

"I'm Jim. That's a beautiful tree," Jim said, looking directly at Eduardo.

"It's so cold out," Eduardo said. "May I offer you something hot to drink, Jim?" The word hot seemed to reverberate throughout the room.

"I think I'll take you up on that," Jim said.

"Will coffee do? I was brewing a fresh pot while we decorated the tree. Milk? Sugar?"

"Black is fine."

I decided it might be time for me to make my exit. "I've got some filing to do in my office. Nice meeting you, Jim," I said, although he hadn't officially acknowledged my existence.

"B.D., where are you going?" Eduardo asked. "Sit down."

I sat. I felt like a dog: a large, warm body with nothing to contribute to the conversation.

Eduardo came out from the kitchen carrying a tray with three mugs. He placed it on the coffee table, handed one mug to Jim, another to me, and took the third for himself, settling into a chair opposite his gentleman caller. "Do you live around here, Jim, or are you just visiting the city?"

"I live over on Greenwich Avenue."

"How wonderful," Eduardo said. "We're practically

neighbors. Perhaps you'd like to come to my annual holiday fête? A few films, lots of food, and a little bit of caroling; you can come for part of it or all of it."

"Well, I'm not sure," Jim said. "Though it certainly sounds like fun."

"It's for old friends and new friends," Eduardo said, with a slight emphasis on new. He leaned forward. "Please, let me print out an invitation for you."

While Eduardo was out of the room, Jim and I sipped our coffee in silence. I tried to determine if he was the kind of man who would appreciate seeing Eduardo in a long-sleeved red robe trimmed with white fur, a replica of the outfit worn by Rosemary Clooney in the finale of *White Christmas*.

The coffee was finished, business cards were exchanged, and Jim went on his way. Eduardo took the mugs back to the kitchen, while I gathered up the tissue that had cradled the ornaments since the previous year.

"Do you think Jim will come to the fête, B.D.?" Eduardo asked.

I didn't know how to answer. Sometimes it was easier to believe in Santa Claus and angels than in human beings. While the holidays held the potential for happiness, it was easy to hope for too much. I enjoyed celebrating quietly, and alone. Some people had a hard time accepting that I preferred sipping hot cider and piecing together a reproduction of a painting of angels while Christmas carols played on the radio.

I knew that Eduardo had some quiet holiday rituals too. One was to go to the General Post Office at 32th Street and Eighth Avenue and select some letters to Santa. He would try to fulfill the wishes of the letter writers. At the stroke of midnight on Christmas Eve, he would share a toast of cider with a few of his closest friends, a tradition carried over from his childhood in Argentina. And on Christmas Day, before going out to dinner, he dressed up in a Santa suit, complete with white moustache and beard, and went to a city homeless shelter with a sack of oranges, chocolate bars, clothing, and toys.

Chapter 7

I was riding home on the subway, reading Sarah Waters' *Tipping the Velvet*. After the guy who'd been sitting next to me got off the train, I felt a gentle jolt and glanced up to give the requisite glare. I never did, for I quickly realized that the woman who had slid across the seats to my side was no ordinary commuter.

She was wearing a black down jacket, a black watch cap, and black leather pants.

"Luvly book, that," she said with a British accent.

I smiled. "Yes it is. Are you on vacation?"

She nodded.

"First trip to the States?"

"Yes."

"How do you like New York so far?"

"Well," she said, "I'm liking it much better now."

She had beautiful brown eyes.

"I'm Jean," she said.

"And I'm B.D. It's sort of a nickname."

"So, B.D., what can you tell me about the women's scene around here? Are there any dances?"

"The community center has a women's dance once a month," I said. "How long are you going to be here?"

"I'm in New York for another week, then I'm going to San Francisco."

"The women's dance won't be until the end of the month," I said. The subway doors opened and I quickly checked the station sign. "Two more stops, then I have to get off," I said.

"My stop is the next one. Could we have coffee or something?"

"Sure. Do you have a sweet tooth?" I asked hopefully, thinking of the pastries at Café aux Camélias.

"Not really."

So I took Jean to the brightly lit Broadway Blue Plate. It was practically empty but held the promise of the white-haired men and blue-rinsed women who rise with the sun and come in search of the breakfast specials. As Jean and I shrugged off our coats and slid into opposite sides of a padded mustard-colored booth, the waiter wiped the gold-veined Formica tabletop between us with a damp cloth.

"The lemonade is actually very good here," I said to Jean. "They make it with fresh lemons."

"I think I'll have tea," Jean said. "I always have a cup of tea before bed."

Jean's long-sleeved Carhartt henley shirt hinted at a slender, sinewy body, and it was clear to me that although her clothing had been chosen for comfort, she was aware that certain people might find it pro-vocative.

We talked about our jobs. Jean told me she worked for a government agency. I explained that I was a bridal consultant.

"Working with brides-to-be seems like an odd sort of job for a dyke," Jean said.

"I agree. It's a little bit like being a resistance fighter inside enemy headquarters. It really helps that my boss has a drag queen alter ego."

"Do you ever get the feeling that a client might be making a mistake?"

"In terms of the man she's marrying? Or because my gaydar is picking up something?"

"Both," Jean said.

"Sometimes my instinct tells me there's something about the groom. But I've never sensed a latent lesbian among the brides-to-be."

"How do you feel about one-night stands, B.D.?" Jean asked.

After my experience with Sylvia, I was aware of the potential for either success or disaster in Jean's question. I thought for a moment, then decided to opt for an honest reply, even if it killed my chances.

"In theory, I'm in favor of one-night stands," I said. "But I'm afraid in practice I'm not very good at them. I have to say, though, that the few one-night stands I have had have been with men."

"Have you just come out, then?" Jean asked.

"Pretty much."

"You're not dating anyone?"

"Not really. There is someone I'm attracted to, but we're just friends, and besides, she's in a relationship."

"That's a hard one," Jean said.

"What about you?"

Jean smiled. "Oh, I'm a very old dyke," she said. "I've been out for a long time; I've had to fight for my life. I just broke up with the woman I've been with for the last five years. So I'm back in the dating scene. With one-night stands, it can be difficult to know what you're getting into. Women who expect me to be really butch are disappointed."

I tried to figure out what that meant, and whether it was meant for me.

"Maybe we could have a drink later on in the week,"

Jean said. "I'd like to see the Stonewall Inn; I understand it's still there."

"OK," I said, writing my name and phone number on
Jean's subway map.

~~~

Jean called me from a club the following night. "Hello,
B.D. I'm at the She-Wolf's Lair, but not much is happening here."

"It may be too early," I told her. "From what I've
heard, the She-Wolf's Lair doesn't start filling up until
after midnight." I didn't know what to do. "My apartment's a mess," I said.

I met Jean outside my apartment building and we
walked over to Riverside Park, shivering in the night air.
There was no question of our actually going into the
park, of course—it was dark out—so we sat on a park
bench along Riverside Drive. Before long an elderly
woman wearing a black Persian lamb pillbox hat joined
us. She paid no attention to us, as she was engrossed in
a bitter conversation with herself, but it was a bit hard
for us to ignore her entirely.

We went back to my apartment, which is one of
those New York City dwelling spaces with windows
that remain open throughout the year, as the heat
blasting from the radiator turns the space into a
sauna. Within minutes of coming through the door,
we began removing unnecessary clothing. Since piles
of paper and books occupied both chairs, we had to sit
on my bed.

Jean didn't give me time to be nervous, because the
second we sat down she put her arms around me and
kissed me.

I said, "I've never done this before."

"That's all right," Jean replied. "I have."

Once we were entirely free of fabric Jean held my breasts and lowered her head. As I savored the luxury of her lips on my nipple, I gently placed my palms over her sweet, sand dollar breasts. Our skin, already misted with the sweat from the day, became slick with the sweat of sex. We didn't say much, but when her hand slid down and her finger slid in, Jean smiled at me and whispered, "This is why I'm a dyke."

She stroked me with her thumb in a rhythm that was a pleasurable variation on my own familiar pattern. I lay quiescent, meditating on the motions of her fingers as though I might have to diagram them the following day. The sounds I heard seemed separate from me, although I knew I was the source of them. I thought about women in books who could come at a touch, a breath, a look, a word. Why was I always the tortoise and never the hare? But the tortoise won the race, eventually, so maybe that wasn't a good metaphor. And what happened to the hare that made him the loser? I was thinking too much. I wondered how much time had passed, if Jean was bored, or would like to give her fingers a rest.

"I'm sorry," I said. "I'm a little nervous. I can come when I'm by myself, but a lot of the time I use a vibrator."

Jean propped herself up on one elbow, leaning her head into her hand, and resting the damp fingertips of her other hand on the swell of my stomach. "We can use your vibrator if you want to," she said.

I shook my head. "I really want your fingers touching me, not a machine." I put my hand over hers and moved it down again.

A few minutes later I pushed Jean's hand away and rolled on top of her. I circled each nipple several times with my tongue, then slid my hands to her hips and my head between her thighs.

Later, I would lie to people who asked me if I'd practiced safe sex, and tell them I did. But at this moment, my need was my world.

I took Jean's sighing and moaning as evidence that, even if I had no idea of what I was doing, I was doing something right.

When Jean grew quiet I lifted myself up over her body, then lay down again, propping myself up on my elbows. I felt the way I feel at the end of my first day in a foreign country—a place familiar and strange at the same time. I was exhausted yet wakeful.

As we lay heart to heart, her face softened into a kind of beauty that no one else saw—not her boss, the man at the corner newsstand, or the stranger on the bus. I wondered then if this happened every time, with every woman.

———

If it had been up to me, I would have kept Jean in bed the whole week, but after all, it was her vacation.

On the night we had dinner in a tiny Middle Eastern restaurant, we looked at each other so intensely our silence seemed almost a siren, and I was surprised the other patrons didn't stare.

On the day I called in sick, we took a round trip on the Staten Island ferry. I loved the view coming back toward Manhattan. The buildings seemed all pressed together, without space. I told Jean it reminded me of a scene in an illuminated manuscript. Then we went shopping in the Village. Jean bought me a t-shirt and I bought her a ring she'd admired—a plain, silver band inlaid with a black enamel triangle.

On Jean's last day in New York, we sat on a bench in Riverside Park and watched the Hudson River flow by. Jean kissed me, and even as some small part of me worried we might be attacked, a much bigger part of me, stocking up for the cold time ahead, wanted to have as much of her as possible.

Jean cried first, smearing tears over her cheeks with the back of her hand.

That was all I needed to set me off. "I'm afraid no one will ever love me," I sobbed.

"B.D. you'll always be my baby dyke."

I liked the sound of that. It wasn't like my mother saying I would always be her baby when I was no longer a baby, either physically or mentally. But Jean would always be my first time and later lovers would not change that.

Chapter 8

Bridget and Natalie had just returned from celebrating their third anniversary, and Bridget had asked me to meet them for brunch. Natalie had invited Maxine. Although Bridget and Natalie had been dating for three years, this was their first trip together, for Bridget preferred to go to places where there was at least the possibility of a coup d'état, while Natalie sought the coup of a bargain. Rarely, if ever, did these objectives coincide in one location. Finally they compromised, which meant, I gathered, that Bridget had acceded to Natalie's wishes this time with the understanding that at some unspecified future point Natalie would proffer some sort of quid pro quo. And, as a practical matter, retail is easier to get to than revolution, especially if all you have is a long weekend.

"So what did you do up in Maine?" I asked.

"I dared Natalie to try the lobster at McDonald's. And she shopped for shirts for me at the L.L.Bean store after she tore my favorite one," Bridget said. She turned to Natalie. "I would have taken it off if you asked. You didn't have to rip it."

I forced myself to swallow a bit of Belgian waffle while

I digested the implications of what Bridget had just said. There is no trouble that cannot be cured by a Belgian waffle.

"I told you I'd buy you a new shirt to replace it and I did," Natalie said.

"But it had been washed to just the right amount of softness," Bridget said. "The new shirts will be scratchy and I'll have to start all over again."

"Who took care of your cats?" I asked.

"My friend Dana. Alice B. coughed up a really huge hairball on the bathroom floor, and Dana stepped on it when she got up to pee in the middle of the night."

"You had quite a few hairballs too," Natalie said, smirking at Bridget, who blushed and frowned, shaking her head.

I imagined grinding Natalie's face into her eggs Benedict. "How was the weather?" I asked, and glanced up from my plate across the table.

Maxine didn't seem to have much of an appetite. Slumped in her chair, she was sculpting her scrambled eggs with her fork.

"We have more important things to discuss than the weather, B.D. I hear you finally got some," Bridget said.

"Where did you hear that?" I suddenly felt quite shy about Jean. But since I continually speculated about Bridget's sex life, it seemed only fair to allow her to inquire about mine.

"The lesbian community is like those tribes that live hundreds of miles apart, with no apparent means of communication, yet somehow they know everything that's going on with each other," Bridget said.

"We ran into Eduardo on Christopher Street," Natalie told me.

When I'd returned to work after my first night with Jean, Eduardo had looked at me, put his hands on his

80

hips and declared, "B.D., I'm glad to see you finally have that W.L.L."

"What?"

"Well Laid Look. It's clear what you did last night."

I didn't have to say anything; my flaming face said it all.

Now, at the brunch table, I felt my face go red again.

"Come on, B.D.," Bridget said. "Spill. Who is she? Where did you meet her? What does she look like? And when do I get to meet her?"

"You won't be able to," I said. "She's already gone back to England."

"I've found an ocean to be very useful in terms of managing a relationship," Maxine remarked.

I ignored her. "Her name is Jean," I said. "She lives in London, and was here on vacation. I met her in the subway."

"You picked up someone in the subway?" Clearly, Natalie did not approve.

"Actually, Jean picked me up," I said.

"B.D., I'm very happy for you," Bridget said. "It's a shame that it was just a fling."

"Why?" Maxine asked. "What's wrong with a fling? I have them all the time."

"That's fine for you," Bridget said. "but I'd like to see B.D. with someone who will stick around."

I thought I knew why. Bridget assumed that if I were involved with someone, my crush on her would disappear. She was wrong, of course. My experience with Jean made me want Bridget all the more. As Erica had suggested the night of our Scotch-tasting adventure, I was in training, preparing myself for the marathon that really mattered. Jean had been a sprint; I was ready for a longer race.

Chapter 9

The white limousine stopped in front of the McKnight house. It wasn't the home Bridget had left when she was seventeen; the McKnights had moved since then. Eduardo and I walked up the cement path to the door with its fake forsythia wreath. Mrs. McKnight opened it before we could ring the bell. "Nancy can't decide which earrings to wear," she said, ushering us inside.

"I thought we all agreed on the diamonds," I said.

"Yes, but last night at the rehearsal dinner her grandmother gave her a pair of pearl earrings."

I caught a glimpse of a porcelain figurine-filled living room as I started up the stairs to the second floor. It could have passed for a Lladro museum.

"Hurry up, B.D.," Eduardo muttered. He loathed Lladro.

Nancy looked very nice in the dress Natalie had selected for her. Her hair and makeup had been professionally done. After she tried on both pairs of earrings for me, I suggested that she stick with the diamonds as we had originally planned.

Bridget was already at the church. Natalie had not been invited. "My mother was freaked out when she heard I would be wearing a tux," Bridget had told me. "I didn't want to have to deal with her reaction if I asked to bring my girlfriend."

When we arrived at the church, I was pleased to note that Bridget looked as good as I had imagined she would. I didn't get a chance to compliment her, for she was talking to the wedding guests.

Everyone was finally seated and the ceremony began.

Because of my job, I've been to more weddings than most people. Yet I still find the wedding itself, whether in a church or synagogue, backyard or country club, to be very moving.

When the pastor asked Nancy if she took Scott to be her lawfully wedded husband, I wasn't the only one who held my breath for what seemed to be an interminable interval. After Nancy said, "I do," the entire bridal party, including the bride and groom, as well as the congregation, seemed more relaxed.

Chapter 10

Being subservient can get on your nerves. I closed the apartment door behind me, grateful that I'd left the rest of humanity outside. I wondered how married people managed, when they came home growling and found yet another person expecting something, needing something.

I kicked off my pumps, unzipped, then dropped my pants and rolled down my pantyhose. Within minutes I had shed my work clothes and changed into sweatpants and a t-shirt. Sliding my feet into a pair of rubber flip-flops, I shuffled into the kitchen.

I fed Truffle, and started boiling water for spaghetti. Then I opened a jar of sauce, spilling half of it into a pot. Sometimes I eat at the sink right out of the pot, but tonight I had junk mail to read, so I transferred the piles of paper from the table to my bed and took out a place-mat.

While I waited for the water to boil, I reviewed the day. Linda Pennie's wedding was only weeks away but she had yet to select a gown, claiming she wanted to lose more weight.

The menu for the Greve-Lesser wedding was proving

to be problematic—between the bride and the groom and their immediate families, a variety of food allergies had to be addressed: lactose intolerance, wheat products, peanuts, strawberries and cherries.

The water was boiling. I stirred in a handful of spaghetti.

Then there was Alexandra Nitschke, soon to be Alexandra Nitschke-Voloch. Alexandra had amazing hair—setter red, wavy, Lady Godiva-length tresses. It was easy to picture Alexandra as a faerie queene bride, flowers twined through her rippling curls, or in a square-necked, flowing gown with sleeves that hung like icicles below her wrists, perhaps a long, hooded cape buttoned to her shoulders. A creamy brocade, with pearl and gold bead embroidery, the lining of the sleeves and cape a golden silk, and a diadem on her head in lieu of a veil. But Alexandra wanted something a little less dramatic. And though she lacked imagination in terms of her apparel, she had a unique vision of what she wanted the theme of her bridal shower to be.

"I want a tool shower," Alexandra said.

When she announced that, Eduardo swallowed his coffee and put the cup down gently, as if there were nothing unusual about the request.

"You see, I don't wear lingerie, and my kitchen is pretty well stocked. But Eugene and I want to buy a little fixer-upper, and I don't have many tools."

I made a note in the file: "Wrench for a wench; True Value instead of Tiffany's." I loved the concept. I pictured the invited guests, accustomed to shopping for wineglasses and cookware, inquiring about drill bits instead. I imagined a set of screwdrivers wrapped up in paper with lacy pink parasols and a curly bow.

"Well, give us a day or two to come up with some options," Eduardo said, rising to show Alexandra out.

When he returned I said, "You handled that very well, Eduardo."

"Would you like to take this one on, B.D.? I think it's more in your line of experience, don't you?"

"Because I'm a lesbian? For someone who plays with gender the way you do, I think you're being a little—provincial, Eduardo."

He started to reply, but I raised my hand. "I'll do it. Not because I'm a lesbian, but because I like the idea."

Now I put the pasta on a plate, poured the sauce over it, sprinkled a large tablespoon full of Parmesan cheese on top, and sat down at the table, wondering if Home Depot offered a bridal registry.

I opened the invitation with Natalie's return address. I recognized the stationery as one that Eduardo and I often recommended our clients use for their thank-you notes.

The details were handwritten in what appeared to be a fountain pen. "You are invited for brunch at the home of Natalie Lamont to celebrate Bridget's birthday, April 1 at noon."

I wondered what I would wear. Jeans seemed too casual.

I put the invitation aside and went on to the first of several mail order catalogs. Initially, they didn't look worth perusing: stained glass lamps in the shapes of a rooster and a swan; an elaborately framed still life of a violin, some sheet music, and a bunch of pink daisies; a sculpture of a leering rabbit with one bent ear. But I became intrigued by the simulated security camera, the turquoise palm tree CD holder, and the Victorian birdcage, complete with decorative bird. When I saw the lampshade with the Dallas Cowboys logo, I decided to order one for Bridget for a birthday present. According to the description, I could choose from any NFL, NBA, AL, or NL team logo.

I tried to recall the names of the New York football teams. One was the Giants, the other was—the Jets. Which would Bridget prefer? I had no idea. Then I remembered that the Jets were a gang in *West Side Story*. I figured Bridget would appreciate the Broadway tie-in.

I left the page with the lampshades open and turned to the latest Victoria's Secret catalog. I always felt a little guilty looking through one of these. Somehow it just didn't seem right for a lesbian—even a femme—to have a Victoria's Secret charge account. I felt as if I was letting lesbians all across the country down by wanting to look like the models. From puberty on, I had yearned to be a woman in a perfume ad. I tried dressing my peasant body in tiny floral print dresses, but of course it didn't work.

People kept asking me why I didn't just forget about Bridget. Her friend Dana and I had been exchanging emails, and I had come to think of Dana as she-who-explains-Bridget. Dana checked in with me on a regular basis, monitoring the status of my affections.

"Are you over Bridget yet?" she would ask.

"I don't turn my feelings on and off like a faucet, Dana."

"Give it up, B.D.. It's never going to happen."

Erica, on the other hand, had permanently endeared herself to me by advocating cautious optimism. "You never know what's going to happen, B.D.," she said. "Natalie and Bridget could be together forever, or they could break up next year."

Recently, Eduardo had confided an uplifting tale. "Honey, I knew Sean for twenty years before we finally got together, and we weren't even speaking to each other for eight of them. Never give up, B.D. Walk on, walk on with hope in your heart."

But Dana told me, "I know Bridget's game, because I've played it. It's very flattering to have someone have a crush on you; it's good for your ego. So you string them along."

—*mm*—

I picked up the phone on the third ring.

"Bambi." The voice was a drawn-out whisper, almost otherworldly.

"Hi, Renee." I didn't ask how she was. With Renee that question was guaranteed to spark a thirty-minute monologue.

"Did you know there's a company that arranges trips especially for lesbians?"

"Yes," I said. "In fact, I'm sure there's more than one."

"There was an article in today's paper. I had to call you."

"Thanks," I said.

"The company is called Olivia."

"Yes, I get their brochures in the mail."

"Bambi."

"Yes?"

"I just wanted to say I'm sorry."

"About what?"

"I've only just realized how traumatic my wedding must have been for you."

Renee had gotten married at City Hall, while I was traveling with my parents. "I was very happy for you, Renee." I'd always liked Renee's husband.

"You were in love with me, weren't you, Bambi?"

My instinct was to blurt out, *God, no!*, but I tried to think of something a little more tactful. "I've always cared for you as a friend, Renee, but it was never more than that."

"I understand that you need to see it that way," Renee said. "Are you dating anyone yet?"

89

"No."

"What about that woman you sent me the picture of?"

Bridget's photograph had appeared in one of the lesbian and gay free weekly newspapers. She was scheduled to speak at a meeting of GLIB—Gay and Lesbian Insurance Brokers.

"Oh, we're just friends."

"She looks very strong, Bambi. Very grounded. You need that."

"I know," I said. "Do you want to hear something weird? She only has music on her home answering machine; there's no outgoing message. And the words to the music aren't in English—it sounds like Russian or something."

"You should read Jung on the trickster figure," Renee said. Renee didn't go in for light reading. "My Xanax is kicking in. Good night, Bambi."

I sighed as I hung up the phone. Then I brushed my teeth, put on my Victoria's Secret pink plaid pajamas with the fake boxer short bottoms, and climbed into bed.

The phone rang again. I wondered if it might be Renee, calling back. She did that sometimes. I picked up the receiver almost fearfully.

"Hello?"

"Hey, B.D.!" Bridget's voice was as rich and warm as a cup of hot chocolate, topped with whipped cream.

"Hey yourself."

"Did you get the invitation to my party?"

"Yes, I got it today."

"You're coming, aren't you?"

"Of course," I said.

"I really want you to be there, B.D. I don't have many friends."

"But Bridget, every time we go someplace together you end up running into someone you know."

"I know lots of people, but they're not my friends. I need you to be my friend."

You and everyone else I've ever been attracted to, I thought, while I said, "I am your friend." As I said this, the hand that wasn't holding the receiver to my ear slipped under the waistband of my pajama bottoms and rested on my crotch. "Hey, I saw your picture in the paper."

"God, that was such an awful photograph. Don't show it to anyone, OK, B.D.?"

"OK," I said. The chances of Bridget running into Renee or my cousin Sarah were pretty small.

"I should let you go to sleep," Bridget said. "Good night, Bambino."

"Good night," I said.

When I closed my eyes, the screen lit up and the feature began. When Bridget's face appeared, a voice whispered, "It's just a fantasy," and I lifted my face for her kiss.

Chapter 11

Sunlight washed over the white walls, furniture and rugs of Natalie's apartment, suffusing the space in brilliant white light. I wondered if I had died and was on my way to wherever.

Bridget's birthday brunch was a very exclusive gathering. Besides the hostess and the guest of honor, there were only two other people—Maxine Huff, and myself.

While we were waiting for Maxine to arrive, Natalie gave me a tour of her apartment. She showed me the mini-hydroponic garden in which she grew vegetables and herbs. She demonstrated how she could watch the Food Network while working out on the treadmill that was part of her compact yet impressive set of exercise equipment.

"I have a personal trainer who comes in three times a week."

"Natalie is very refined," Bridget said. "She can only sweat around people she really trusts."

When Natalie ushered me into her bedroom, I tried not to think about what went on in there.

I love looking at photographs—fine art, snapshots, old family albums. So it was natural for me to want to take a closer look at the large black and white images of nudes that were hanging on the wall, and the contents of the small but tasteful frames placed on the bedside table.

I blushed when I realized the nudes were all Natalie. The two photographs by the bed were of Maxine, and Natalie with Maxine. I couldn't help but wonder if it ever bothered Bridget to have Maxine looking over her shoulder, as it were, in Natalie's bed. But maybe she was so focused on what she was doing that she didn't think about it. Maybe it turned her on. Maybe they only did it in total darkness.

Maxine finally arrived. She was wearing a black leather jacket and mirrored aviator sunglasses. She complained to no one in particular, "Why do they have to come out to me? Why don't they come out to someone else? Today was the third time this month that a student invited me to her apartment for dinner. Do they think I don't have a life?"

"Is that why you're late?" asked Natalie.

"I'm a teacher. I have a responsibility to accommodate my students if they ask to see me. But once, just once, I wish they'd ask me about something on the syllabus. I've been listening to coming out stories for seven years now. The topic's getting old."

"You're getting old too," Bridget told her.

"Hey, it's your birthday," Maxine replied. "Do you know that a couple of students started a zine about me? The Max Zine."

"Have you seen it? What's it like?" I asked.

"It's a bunch of erotic poems, stories, and cartoons."

"It's tough, being a sex object," Bridget said.

"How would you know?" Natalie asked her.

"I think it's an honor to be the inspiration for that kind of tribute," I said.

"Somehow they found a photograph of me that was

taken back when I was living in the feminist commune—wearing overalls and feeding baby goats."

"You're just embarrassed about those overalls," Bridget said. "The baby goats are really cute."

"You have to give whoever found it some credit for their research skills," I added.

"Bribery is a more likely factor," Maxine replied.

"Of an ex," Bridget said. "You've got so many."

"Are you going to take off your jacket or not?" Natalie asked.

"The most recent volume is a paper doll book," Maxine said darkly, hands jammed into her pockets. "With clothes. And underwear. And—accessories."

"Sunglasses?" I guessed.

"Yes, they had those too."

Bridget laughed.

I tried to find the joke.

"One of the accessories is a harness with a dildo in it," Bridget explained.

"Isn't that clever!" I exclaimed.

"No, it's not," Maxine snapped. "How did you know about that?" she asked Bridget.

"Natalie has a lifetime subscription to that 'zine," Bridget replied.

"Which you gave me as a present," Natalie said.

"Which you asked for."

Maxine shrugged off her jacket and removed her sunglasses, and I had my first chance to really see her eyes.

As far as I'm concerned, the eyes have it. Not that I don't appreciate the other parts of a woman's body, but the eyes—when I looked into Maxine's, my clothes dissolved like cotton candy on my tongue and I believed she knew all my secrets, especially the ones I hadn't gotten around to telling my therapist. But Maxine didn't trade information; she didn't offer up any secrets of her own. Not so much as a hint of one.

Bridget opened her birthday champagne with an ease and authority that I found arousing. We toasted her, then sat down to an appetizer of wild mushrooms and goat cheese galettes.

Natalie asked me if I had ever designed a bridal gown.

"I did study fashion design," I replied, "and I do freelance occasionally. In fact, I recently did a dress based on one of my favorite Barbie doll outfits, the strapless black evening gown with the net flounce at the ankles."

"I was only interested in taking Barbie's clothes off," Bridget said.

"I never played with dolls; I played with real girls," Maxine remarked.

"I want to hear about the wedding dress," Natalie said.

"I made the dress in white lamé and netting dotted with brilliants at the ankles and above the breasts. The headpiece echoed the flounce at the bottom; it looked a little like the bride was wearing a lampshade on her head. And she wore over-the-elbow white satin gloves. I almost got mentioned in the Vows column in the Sunday *New York Times*.

"Really? What happened?"

"Oh, that was the week the female CEO of a major stock brokerage house married the man who wrote that bestseller on goddess worship. The ceremony was held in the reptile house at the zoo."

"I think I remember reading about that," Natalie said.

"And I was interviewed by a reporter from a bridal magazine who was writing an article about bridal consultants dream weddings," I said. "I told her I wanted to get married in Hawaii, on the beach, wearing vintage Hawaiian shirts."

"Well, that was prescient of you," Maxine said.

"Actually, at the time I wasn't even out to myself."

Maxine put her hands over her ears. "I don't want to hear another coming out story."

"Sorry," I said. "Anyway, the reporter told me she couldn't use it. She said it would be bad for business; it might give women ideas. She asked what would happen to the wedding gown designers and manufacturers and the bridal shop owners if people started to get married in things like Hawaiian shirts?"

—*m*—

As she served the main course—tornedos of poached salmon with lemon rice—Natalie told me she was going hunting for morels with Maxine.

I had no idea what morels were, but I played along. "Where?"

"It's a secret."

"I won't tell."

"Well, we don't know where we're going and we won't find out until we get there," Maxine said.

"We're supposed to meet the leaders in a parking lot, and they'll take us where we're supposed to go," Natalie explained.

"Do you have to synchronize your watches too?" I asked.

Maxine pulled her wallet out of her pocket, opened it, took out a card, and handed it to me. The card informed me that Maxine was a member in good standing of the Park Slope Clitocybes. "The Park Slope Clitocybes sounds like a lesbian softball team," I said.

"Well it's not," said Maxine. "It's a mycological society."

"Mushrooms," Natalie said. "We're learning how to find them and identify them."

97

"Those mushrooms we just ate. They weren't . . ." I thought I could feel my stomach cramping.

"I got those at Balducci's," Natalie reassured me.

"My father told me once that I was going to die from eating mushrooms," Bridget said.

I looked at her, but Natalie continued as though Bridget hadn't spoken.

"It is sort of inconvenient, not knowing where we're going," Natalie said. "It makes it hard to pack."

"Pack?" I said.

"We're going to be away for a weekend," Maxine explained.

"Don't you have to make hotel reservations?"

"We're going camping."

"Bugs, bears, bathroom-in-the-woods camping?" I tried to picture Natalie squatting behind a bush. "This has to be an April Fool's joke," I said.

The meal had been spectacular so far, and I was looking forward to seeing what Natalie was going to bring forth by way of a birthday cake. I admit to being a traditionalist when it comes to birthday and wedding cakes. I love breaking the surface of the white icing to sink into the softer cream beneath, all buttery and sweet and sticking to the roof of my mouth, though not as much as peanut butter. I prefer a corner piece, or one with a rose. I wasn't expecting Natalie to have my very favorite kind of cake; she would probably agree with Eduardo, who complains that my taste is vulgar. Still, I was disappointed when she appeared carrying plates with little cookie cups piled high with some creamy substance and topped with a strawberry.

"It's a fool," Natalie said. "For April Fool's Day."

Bridget's didn't even have a candle in it.

After Natalie had cleared the table, Bridget opened her presents. Maxine had given Bridget a signed copy of her new book, *Lesbian Bed Death and Resurrection*.

"Thanks, Maxine," Bridget said. "I'm sure I'll find this very interesting."

When she saw the lampshade, Bridget laughed. She looked at me and began to snap her fingers. "When you're a Jet, you're a Jet all the way, from your first cigarette to your last dying day," she sang.

Natalie glared at her.

"I'm going to put this in my office," Bridget said. "Thanks, B.D."

I looked over at Natalie. She looked back at me. "I am the gift," she said.

—⚡—

At the door, Bridget held out her arms to me. I embraced her gingerly, afraid of holding her a bit too tightly for a heartbeat too long. I stepped back before she could pull away, but she let her hands rest lightly on each side of my body, sliding them up and down in an absentminded way.

"We didn't sing 'Happy Birthday,'" I said.

"That's OK," Bridget replied. "I'm just glad you were here, B.D. That's the really important thing."

Chapter 12

"B.D., were you going to let me go out like this?"

"You look wonderful," I said.

"My lipstick's smeared."

Valentine stood in front of the mirror. I had just finished zipping up her dress. Earlier that day she had been Eduardo, wedding consultant to parvenus and arrivistes and my boss, but now she was the one and only Valentine Starlight.

I had seen drag so bad it was actually good, knowing all the while it was drag. But when Eduardo was in Valentine mode, he made me forget.

The paradox fascinated me. As Valentine, Eduardo became the glamorous woman I wished I could be, with the kind of body favored by fashion designers—slender, no hips, a small ass, and negligible breasts. Of course, in Valentine's case, what breasts there were, came courtesy of padding and other tricks.

I loved Valentine's outfits: the head-to-toe attention to detail, the color coordination and accessories.

"What are you going to sing?" I asked, although Valentine would, in fact, be lip-synching.

"I'm not sure. I feel sort of *melancólico* tonight, B.D.

I've been looking for Mr. Right but finding Mr. Right Now. But I know my audience is expecting something big, something bright, something Broadway."

I sighed. "Well, I'm a little confused right now. When Bridget walked through the door of that bridal salon, I thought I'd found the special person I'd been hoping for. The more time I spend with her, the more I feel a connection between us. I fantasize about her all the time. But yesterday, at Bridget's birthday party, Maxine was so . . . I wanted her too, but in a different way. With Bridget, I look at her and the world stops, there's just the two of us."

"Tony and Maria at the gym dance in *West Side Story*," Valentine said.

"Well, yes. When you put it that way, it seems kind of corny, but it doesn't feel corny when it's happening."

"And with Maxine?"

"With Maxine it's more like Luke Skywalker going into the cave in *The Empire Strikes Back*. I feel compelled, but a little scared. I dreamed about Maxine last night. She was a black cat."

"How could you tell it was Maxine?" Valentine asked.

I thought for a minute. "The eyes. I looked into the cat's eyes and I knew it was Maxine."

Valentine held up a different earring next to each ear. "Which ones should I wear?"

"The short jet dangles," I said. "Am I depraved, Valentine? Wanting both Bridget and Maxine?"

"B.D., remember President Carter lusted in his heart. You can desire as many women as you want. You're not depraved, you've just been deprived—a little Jill-in-the-Box who's finally been set free."

—*m*—

After Valentine went off to do her show, I met Annalise and Ellen at a Greek diner. As we drank coffee from white cups so thick our biceps got a workout with every sip, Annalise advised me on how to be a proper lesbian, a lesbian who could be recognized as a lesbian by other lesbians. I borrowed a pen from Ellen and took notes on a napkin.

"First, cruising is a subtle art, B.D.," Annalise said. "Stop with the human periscope imitation. I can tell when a butch walks by the window just by watching you."

"It's not good for your neck," Ellen said. "You could give yourself whiplash."

"Now for your cultural education. You have to see *The Hunger*."

"Isn't that a vampire film?"

"Yes, but there's a sex scene with Susan Sarandon and Catherine Deneuve."

"But I don't like scary films. I was sixteen years old before I watched *The Wizard of Oz* straight through. I used to turn off the TV the minute the Wicked Witch of the West came on," I said.

"B.D., it's Susan Sarandon and Catherine Deneuve!"

"Then you have to rent *Salmonberries*," Ellen said.

"Didn't that get terrible reviews?"

"Just fast forward to k.d. lang's nude scene and press the pause button."

"Why doesn't someone just put all these scenes on one DVD?"

"You have seen *Desert Hearts*, haven't you?" Annalise asked.

I sighed and shook my head.

"What!" Ellen cried.

"You've never seen *Desert Hearts*?" Annalise said.

They immediately began to lay out the whole film for me, scene for scene, and on occasion, line for line and word for word.

"It's pouring rain, and Cay knocks on the car window, motions the professor to roll down the window."

"So the professor rolls it down partway and Cay says—"

"'Roll it all the way down.'"

"So she does and Cay puts her head in."

"And she kisses the professor's cheek." Annalise demonstrated on Ellen.

"Then they really kiss."

They demonstrated again. Then they looked at each other for a moment.

"And Cay says, 'We don't have to stop.'"

"And the professor says, 'I do.'"

"Then Cay gets in the car and asks her—" they said the last line in unison "—'Where'd you learn to kiss like that?'"

"Didn't you just buy a DVD player?" Ellen asked. "What are you using it for?"

"I hope you're not watching too many musicals, B.D.," Annalise said. "That's a gay boy thing."

In fact, I was watching girl-on-girl porn films. They had titles like *Girls Night Out, Vol. 34* and featured actresses with names like Kittie Hawk and Goldie Locks. The women had tousled blonde hair and long polished nails that made me a little anxious. Occasionally, their technique seemed hampered by glances up at the camera, as if to say, "How am I doing?" But my body wasn't a film critic. I wasn't sure whether to share this, because I hadn't figured out if Annalise and Ellen were erotic lesbians or pornographic lesbians. As with mushrooms, misidentification could have grave consequences.

So I changed the topic and brought them up to date with the latest antics of what Annalise referred to as "the troika." I provided a complete rundown on Bridget's birthday party, including the menu, and Maxine and Natalie's upcoming camping trip.

"Bridget doesn't seem at all concerned about it," I said. "For her, it's no different than the two of them going shopping at an outlet center for a few hours. You don't suppose that Maxine and Natalie will—well, you know."

"Just think about it, B.D. Suppose you were on a camping trip with Bridget," Annalise said.

That was one of my favorite fantasies. A women's adventure travel group offered a sea kayaking expedition to Baja to watch the migration of the gray whales. I had read and re-read the description of the campsite and the sunrise and moonlight excursions, and envisioned Bridget and me in a kayak built for two, rocking on the water beneath a full moon, marveling at the phosphorescence as we listened to the whales sing. Afterward, ensconced in our tent, what could be easier than to slip from intimacy with the natural world to intimacy with each other? I refused to dwell on my terror of any watercraft smaller than the QE2. Great rewards inspire great sacrifices.

"Maybe they will have separate sleeping bags. Or one big one that zips into two compartments." I knew that such things existed from reading the L.L. Bean catalog. "Besides, we're assuming that Natalie is attracted to Maxine, but we don't know for sure."

"Do you know anyone who's not attracted to Maxine?" Ellen asked.

"I'm not," Annalise said. "You're the only one I want, Muffin Buns."

"Well." I said, "I haven't polled the entire lesbian community, but Maxine does seem to have an effect on a lot of women." Certainly, I had never met anyone else who made me want to howl and dance naked in the moonlight.

I returned to a point that had been the subject of frequent discussion. "Bridget and Natalie seem so different. I just don't understand their relationship."

"B.D., you know how Bridget sees herself, don't you?" Annalise said. "She thinks she's still fresh from the farm even though she's never lived on one."

"OK, I can understand Bridget's attraction to Natalie—she's worldly, elegant, and refined—but then what is Natalie getting out of it?"

"Maybe Natalie sees Bridget as a kind of improvement project," Ellen said.

I recalled a friend from high school, saying of her fiancé, "He's not much now, but wait till you see what I'm going to make of him." The last I'd heard she was working on Husband Number Two. "Natalie does seem to enjoy telling people what to do," I said.

Annalise shook her head. "I don't know Bridget very well, but from what I've seen of her, she doesn't seem like someone who would accept being dictated to."

Chapter 13

Bridget and I were walking around the Village, digesting greasy burgers. She was cruising women; I was cruising pastries.

I paused in front of Black Widows Web.

"I dare you," Bridget said.

"I'm not going in here with you. You'll make fun of me."

"Never. Don't you want me to show you how the spanking paddles work?" Sometimes it was hard to tell when Bridget was kidding.

"Not tonight."

Bridget imitated a chicken.

"Look," I said, "I do not have a problem with going into this store. I just don't feel like going in there this minute."

"Prove it," Bridget said. "Go into the store sometime in the next two weeks, buy something and show me the receipt."

"All right, I will."

mm

In fact, I was a little nervous walking into Black Widows Web. I tried to ease into my exploration of the shop by focusing on the fishnet stockings. I was starting to relax a little when I heard my name.

Maxine was standing in front of a row of floggers, caressing the strands of one of them as if it were hair. She seemed almost approachable, exuding the affability of a panther who has just finished a good meal.

"Hi, Maxine!" I sounded like Minnie Mouse.

"I never would have thought I'd see you here, B.D. Are you looking for anything in particular?"

"Ah—a leather bra and garter belt." At least I had some prior knowledge of lingerie.

"Over there." Maxine motioned to some racks on the other side of the store.

A red-and-blue-haired salesperson walked over as I started hunting for extra-large sizes. "This one is sort of one-size-fits-all. The straps just go down and across your breasts, so cup size doesn't really matter. Why don't you try it on?"

Inside the dressing room, I turned the one-size-fits-all contraption around and around in my hands. Where were my arms supposed to go?

"How's it going, B.D.?" Maxine asked.

"Fine."

"Do you need some assistance? I'll come help you." She had slipped through the curtains before I could make up my mind about whether I wanted her to.

"B.D., why are you wearing a bra while you're trying on a bra?"

I pointed to the reminder about hygiene precautions pasted on the mirror.

"I think that means you should keep your underpants on, like when you're trying on a bathing suit."

"I need something a little more industrial," I said, holding up the garter belt, with its black laces criss-

108

crossing through metal rings to tie at the top. "I couldn't close this."

"You're not supposed to be able to close it," Maxine said. "The laces stay open." She untied and loosened the strings. "Here, step into it."

I pulled the garter belt up to my hips, which were covered by flowered cotton briefs. The left side seam of the underpants had split. To her credit, Maxine didn't laugh at the sight of the black laces spanning a field of pink daisies. She unhooked my bra and slipped the straps off my shoulders in a brisk, clinical manner, then arranged the bands of leather across the center of each breast. We stared at my reflection in the mirror. "Let's see what else is out there," Maxine said.

When I emerged from the dressing room, I found Maxine talking to a small, slender woman wearing a close-fitting leather jacket and leather pants.

"Yvette, this is Bambi Devine, otherwise known as B.D."

"Bambi! How sweet."

"You know, Bambi was a male deer," I said. "My mother was a gender bender ahead of her time." This, of course, was pure bravado. My mother had named me Bambi because she felt me kick during the fawn's first appearance on the big screen. Fortunately, I'd had the sense to hold still while Thumper was on.

"Bambi, dear, would you like to come to a little party I'm having? I found this wonderful kneeler at a church rummage sale. Now that I've refinished it, I want to initiate it and formally integrate it into my dungeon."

"Oh lord," I said.

"That's the spirit," Maxine replied.

"Tell me some of your fantasies," Yvette said. "I might be able to hook you up with someone who will help you act them out."

"Well, I'd like to dress up as Alice in Wonderland and

ride on a drag queen float in the Gay Pride parade," I said.

"Yvette means sexual fantasies, B.D.," Maxine said.

"Oh. In that case, maybe I'll just watch what everyone else is doing, thanks."

"So you like to watch?"

I felt myself blush. "When is the party?"

"Sunday evening."

"Oh, darn! I'm afraid I've already got something on for that night." Bridget and I were going to a special sing-along showing of *The Sound of Music* at Ozmosis. Viewers were encouraged to dress in costume. I was looking forward to this because it gave me a chance to relive my moment of glory at summer camp as Sister Margaretta, one of the nuns who sings "How Do You Solve a Problem Like Maria?" I had rented a nun costume in honor of the occasion. Bridget had been practicing "The Lonely Goatherd" over Natalie's protests.

Thinking of Bridget reminded me that I had to buy something so I could show her the receipt. I walked over to a display case near the cash register. I pointed to a pair of very long, very shiny purple gloves. "Can I see these, please?"

As I worked my fingers into the left glove, Maxine pushed the material up my arm.

"It's awfully tight," I said.

"It's supposed to be."

I wondered whether my blood circulation would be affected. If I wore the gloves too long, would I get gangrene and have to have my arms amputated? How would I ever explain the stumps to my mother?

"I live alone, Maxine. I don't have anyone to help me get these gloves on and off."

"You'll just have to find yourself a slave."

Maxine decided to try on a pair of leather pants.

110

While she was in the dressing room, Yvette came over to me and whispered, "You know what Maxine's thing is, don't you?"

"No, but I have wondered."

"Six weeks, six days, and six hours after the first time she goes to bed with a woman, she tells her she's bored and just wants to be friends."

I wondered if the tsar ever got bored of his Fabergé eggs. I figured I would bore Maxine after six minutes.

I wandered over to a colorful display of dildos. There was even one with glitter.

"You know how when you touch something with glitter you're always finding it on you or around you for days afterward?"

"The glitter's part of the silicon," the salesperson said. "It can't escape."

I was reassured. But, although I was sure my gynecologist would not recommend it, I found I rather liked the idea of a little glitter down there. Not too much—a pinch, as the old recipes say. It could be a nice surprise for someone. "Ooh—you sparkle!" I thought even Maxine might be impressed; for a couple of minutes, at least.

"Do you have a mail order catalog?" I asked.

"B.D., why would you order something through the mail when the store is right here?" Maxine said.

When I saw the large book of nineteenth-century spanking photographs, I remembered Bridget's remark about showing me the paddles. I figured it would serve her right if I gave her the book as a gift. I knew she would blush. But what if she already had it?

Then I saw the stockings. I moved toward them as one might approach a holy vision—in wonder, and some disbelief.

They were thick, black stockings—opaque and sturdy. They made me think of Toulouse Lautrec's paintings of the Moulin Rouge dancers and nineteenth-century erotic photographs. But someone from Hollywood had jazzed up the stockings by topping them with long, thin feathers that arced downward like willow branches.

"That's our last pair," the salesperson said. It was kismet.

—⁓⁓—

On Sunday I proudly showed Bridget the receipt.

"Stockings? You went into Black Widows Web and all you bought was a pair of stockings? B.D., I'm disappointed in you." Bridget wasn't in costume, but seemed unfazed by my nun outfit.

"The stockings have feathers," I said.

Bridget seemed intrigued. "I dated a woman who had a sheer nightie thing with fluff around the top and bottom."

"Marabou feathers," I said. "I think the feathers on my stockings are ostrich feathers."

"Can I see them?"

"No. I bought them to wear in my boudoir."

"So?"

"Didn't you tell me you're monogamous?"

"Oh. Yes, I guess I did."

As we entered Ozmosis, someone announced that the film would be starting in fifteen minutes. A woman standing in the Fiction section turned to her companion. "Oh! They're going to be showing *The Sound of Music* here tonight."

"No. Not even for you," her companion replied.

I walked down the stairs, being careful to lift my skirts. A blond man in lederhosen stared at me.

"Bambi?"

"Harvey!"

We hugged. I explained to Bridget that Harvey and I had been at camp together. "He played Rolfe."

"Oh, look," someone said, "it's the Baroness." And there she was, blonde, tastefully bejeweled, swathed in lamé, and somehow familiar. As she swept by me I said, "Valentine, why didn't you tell me you were going to be here?"

"*Pero querida,* B.D., you make a terrifyingly authentic nun."

Harvey bowed, clicked his heels, and kissed Valentine's hand.

Bridget sang every word of every song. At the end of the film, a man sitting in front of her turned and said, "You should save it for the shower, honey."

"Who do you think you are," I asked. "Placido Domingo?"

In reply he handed me a card announcing the appearance of "The Swizzle Sticks, New York City's queer cabaret ensemble" at the Over the Rainbow Room.

Chapter 14

The wine and cheese segment of the meeting of the Third Thursday Networking, Social and Support Group for Professional Lesbians was well under way when I walked into the Lavender Lounge at the Triangle Inn. I had been advised that TTNSSGPL was a major cruise scene. The highlight of the evening was always Stand and Tell, during which a microphone was passed from table to table, and each woman would stand and introduce herself. When the mike arrived at my table I spilled the contents of my purse onto the floor so that I was busy putting everything back in place as the mike made its way from woman to woman.

It wasn't that I didn't want the professional lesbians to see me; I just didn't want them to know that I was a bridal consultant.

Stand and Tell was followed by another social period. I stood sipping my wine, trying to look approachable. The real estate agent, rushing towards the law firm partner in search of a country home, careened into me, splashing red wine onto my ecru silk blouse, which I had ransomed from the dry cleaner the previous weekend. A woman chose that moment to hand me her card.

"Angel Merse, Dyke Investigator."

"So you—ah—investigate women to find out if they're dykes? There have been times when I would have paid a lot of money for that kind of information." It was the best verbal response I could come up with. I was having trouble with coherence, with remaining upright when my hormones were demanding that I lie down. With her Fra Angelico blue eyes and curly, new-penny red-blonde hair that was guaranteed to drive the most congenial cherub into unheavenly envy, Angel Merse was absolutely adorable, certifiably hot. She was also petite. I felt huge. I had torpedoes for breasts and thighs the diameter of redwood trunks that were buckling like willows in the wind. To save Angel's life, I would have to be the bottom. Lucky for both of us, that's the kind of girl I am.

—*mm*—

Of course, it took a while for Angel and me to get to that point. It didn't happen the way it usually did in all those erotic stories I was always reading. Images of rushing off with her to the nearest bathroom, booking a room at the Triangle Inn, or getting naked in her car in the parking lot flickered on my mental screen, but a more urgent matter demanded my attention. "I have to get some seltzer for this wine stain," I said.

Grabbing the nearest bottle from the refreshments table, I twisted the cap off. Seltzer splattered my hair, face and chest. I patted my face with a napkin while Angel gently dabbed at the damned spot on my left breast, just above my bra cup. As my nipples began flaunting their presence beneath the business-like blouse, the red that was slowly disappearing from the silk seeped into Angel's cheeks. It was embarrassing, yet I wished I was showing a little more cleavage.

"I think that should do it," Angel said, dropping her hands and stepping back.

"Thanks."

"My home, office, and cell numbers are on my card, in case you need help with anything else."

Most nights I fantasized about Bridget before falling asleep. But that night I pretended my hands were resting on Angel's curls while her mouth moved across my body like a planchette on a Ouija board, channeling my desire.

Chapter 15

I had decided to spend the day at the beach with Erica. It's a lot of work to go to the beach. First I have to shave my legs, which is always a bit of a production number—I check the backs with a mirror to make sure I haven't missed any spots. Then I have to coat myself with an SPF 30 sun block before I even leave the house. But it gives me an excuse to wear a wide-brimmed blue straw hat with a flowered scarf tied around the base of the crown, the ends falling down to blow in the breeze, if there is one.

We took a train and a taxi to the ferry. As we made our way across the water, I thought about my first trip to Cherry Grove the previous summer. I'd been amazed by how small everything seemed—one-person-wide boardwalk paths; tiny houses squeezed side by side like pieces on a Monopoly board.

We finally arrived at the beach, and settled on the sand, spreading towels and sheets.

"Do you know how long Bridget and Natalie have been together?" Erica asked.

"They celebrated their third anniversary this past February."

"From what I've observed, the time between the third

and fourth years is usually critical in a relationship. If the couple makes it through that—the seventh year is another big one for break-ups. And if they start to think about buying a house together—watch out. There's something about a mortgage that makes people run."

I rolled onto my back and used my hat to cover my eyes.

"Have you ever gone fishing for bass?" Erica asked.

I knew the non sequitur was also a rhetorical question.

"It takes a really long time," Erica said. "You can spend the whole day just waiting. You have to let the bass come up to your bait a couple of times, swim around it, and smell it. You have to be really patient because if you try to reel the bass in too soon you'll lose it."

I saw myself in a rowboat on a lake, wearing a drab jacket and hat, dangling a line down into the water where Bridget, a big, beautiful mermaid with a gleaming bass tail, was swimming. I didn't think about the bait. I don't do worms.

But while I was waiting for Bridget to fall in love with me, there were, so to speak, plenty of other fish in the sea. I sat up and put my hat back on my head.

A few feet away from us a group of young women shared a blanket. Their breasts were bared and they wore boxer shorts. I liked the look, and wondered if I could get away with it.

"How do you think I'd look in boxer shorts?"

"The effect wouldn't be quite the same, B.D.," Erica said. "Your breasts aren't as perky."

I thought of how some of my clients would set their hearts on an unflattering gown, or choose a bridesmaid's dress that looked great on one woman and dreadful on another.

My attention was drawn to someone walking along the water's edge with what looked like a miniature horse.

As they came closer, I saw that it was Angel Merse with a Harlequin Great Dane. The dog's head was level with her shoulders. They came over to where Erica and I were sitting. I looked up at Angel. The combination of the sun and her lustrous curls challenged the efficacy of my sunglasses.

"This is Betty Boop," Angel said.

I let Betty sniff my hand.

Angel shrugged. "The staff at the shelter named her."

Betty grinned and gave up a woof.

"Would you like to join us?" I asked.

"Actually, I'm here on surveillance," Angel said. "Some woman thinks her girlfriend is two-timing her; asked me to check it out."

It occurred to me that in the process of trying to spot one allegedly unfaithful girlfriend, Angel would get to survey a beach full of women. It seemed like a pretty good deal to me.

"I've got to go," Angel said. "We should do dinner or something. I'll call you."

I watched her as she threaded her way through towels and blankets. Then she paused, ostensibly to examine something in the sand.

"Hey," I said to Erica, "I think I see Natalie and Maxine."

"Here, use my binoculars."

"You brought binoculars to the beach?"

"I'm a bird-watcher, B.D."

"Well, there aren't any birds around here right now. If people see me looking through binoculars, they'll think I'm perverted or something."

"Lots of the people in this country already think that. Go for it." Erica handed me a pair of binoculars about the size of a paperback book. I took them, looked around me, then raised them to my eyes and focused on the couple in question.

"It's them," I said. "Maxine is topless." I knew how the archeologist Howard Carter must have felt when he first looked upon the splendor of King Tut's tomb. I also knew that Maxine would be furious if she somehow caught sight of the binoculars. Fortunately, she was engaged in applying sun tan lotion to Natalie's thighs with the painstaking deliberation of an illuminator for whom an entire world can be contained within the outline of a letter. For the sake of Natalie's skin, I hoped that this was just a touch-up job, for at the rate Maxine was going, Natalie's calves would burn into chili peppers before Maxine made her way down to them.

Chapter 16

"No flowers."

"Excuse me, Mrs. Fuchsberg, I'm not quite sure I understand."

"I prefer 'Adele,' Eduardo. I'm telling you that I don't want any flowers at Miriam's wedding. Flowers die. It depresses me when things die."

"But they won't die until after the wedding, Adele."

"Yes, but I'll know that they're going to die."

"I want to be sure I understand what it is that you don't want. You don't want flowers on the tables at the reception. You don't want boutonnières. You don't want bouquets. Even for the bride."

"That's right."

In my file I drew a daisy inside a circle and put a slash across it. I made a note—the bride has to throw something.

"Well," Eduardo said, "We'll have to see what we can come up with. How do you feel about silk flowers?"

"I can't bear anything artificial." Adele pressed her Lee Press On Nails to her breast. Her hair was very blonde, her makeup very heavy, and her skirt very short. I made another note in my file—no matronly gowns for Adele.

After Eduardo showed Adele out, he went directly to his office and closed the door.

I thought that in one of his other lives Eduardo must have been a Victorian maiden who was prone to the vapors. When he finally emerged, I said, "You have to think of it as a challenge to your creativity, Eduardo. You have to look at this as an opportunity to set a trend. You have to ask yourself—what would Martha Stewart do?"

"B.D., I'm going to take a long lunch with Michael at The Queen's Cozy." Michael was the florist behind Mr. Pansy. The Queen's Cozy was a tea and pastry shop that sold tea cozy replicas of Buckingham Palace and Guardsman hats and imported tea towels with pictures of the Royal Family.

"Maybe I'll shop for some boxer shorts," I said, remembering the young women at the beach and thinking of end-of-summer sales.

"All natural fabrics only, and no smiley faces. I'll bring you back a take-out scone with clotted cream and strawberry preserves."

I thought about Maxine's breasts as I walked to Macy's. I thought about them in a respectful way, in the way I contemplate a work of art that inspires and moves me. I wasn't like the guy in front of me in the sandwich line last week, asking the harried man behind the counter for a nice, tender breast, then snorting and honking with his buddy until I wanted to kick him in the shins and scream, "Don't you ever think about anything else you rug-roofed, cigar-smoking creep!" By my standards, Maxine's breasts were perfection.

People were always telling Bridget how lucky she was to have a girlfriend who was a gourmet cook. But from time to time, the pleasures of radicchio, balsamic vinegar, and freshly made pasta would pale and Bridget would call and invite me out for a greasy burger. I was proud that she chose me to be her comrade in her occasional culinary rebellions.

"So B.D., what's new and exciting in your world?" Bridget asked.

"I bought some boxer shorts this afternoon," I said.

"B.D., you constantly surprise me."

I explained about the young women on the beach.

"Well, I hope you'll bring me along for your bare-breasted debut. I'll make sure all your admirers behave themselves. Hey, did you happen to run into Natalie and Maxine while you were at Cherry Grove?"

"Oh, yes, I saw them." I crammed a large French fry into my mouth.

"So, are they having an affair?"

"How should I know?" I couldn't even figure out when I was on a date and when I wasn't. Could I call this dinner a date? I'd consulted Eduardo, but he wasn't much help. "I just hope you know when you're having sex, bebé," he said.

"I just sort of figured that the three of you piled into bed together at least once a week," I said.

Bridget looked horrified. "I'm too much of a WASP."

The only other time Bridget so much as hinted at suspecting that Natalie and Maxine might be more than friends was back at the Fourth of July barbecue hosted by Ellen and Annalise. I was at the kitchen table, feeling the effects of my first strawberry daiquiri and sipping my second. Bridget was sitting to my left, drinking a beer, when Maxine entered the room from the doorway to my right.

"Hey, Maxine," Bridget said "How many girlfriends have we shared?"

I looked from one to the other.

"I don't know," Maxine replied. "Maybe we should each make a list and compare them."

Anyone just listening would have heard only banter, but I could see their eyes—Bridget's cold with anger, Maxine's dark with defiance.

Chapter 17

"Maxine is making me dinner while Natalie is out of town and she'd like you to come too," Bridget said.

"Are you sure? Why didn't she ask me herself?"

"I mentioned that I was going to call you and she asked me to pass along the invitation."

"Should I bring anything?"

"Bread," Bridget said. "Bring plenty of bread."

"Why the emphasis on plenty?" I asked,

"So there will be something we can eat. Think of the bread as self-insurance."

"You exaggerate," I said.

Bridget told me she was going to drive to Maxine's and offered to pick me up outside the subway station near Maxine's apartment building.

With my transportation in place, I began trying to imagine what Maxine's apartment might look like. Would her furniture be leather? Would she have Goddess shrines? Would her bed be a double, queen, or king size? A twin was unthinkable.

The morning of the day of the dinner, I went to Zabar's and bought a large Swiss peasant bread, a large rosemary round, and a large sourdough baguette.

Bridget picked me up at the corner, as arranged.

"Want to stop at McDonald's on the way?" she asked.

"Very funny," I said.

"I am not joking, B.D. I've known Maxine for fifteen years. She can't cook."

—*m*—

Maxine buzzed us up and was waiting at the door to her apartment. She was wearing an attractive wine-colored, button-down shirt with the sleeves rolled up to her elbows, black chinos, and sneakers. "Hi! Come in."

"I brought you some bread," I said, offering the bag.

"One, two—three loaves! Did you bring one for each of us?"

"Actually," I said, "I couldn't make up my mind which kind to get."

"Should I warm them up?"

"You don't have to do that, Maxine," Bridget said.

"It's no trouble; the oven's already on. It'll be nice if the bread is warm."

Bridget sighed and sat down on the sofa that could open up into a futon as Maxine disappeared into the kitchen.

I wandered around the room. The table was square and set for three with woven place mats, stoneware plates and bowls, and paper napkins. There were several bookcases and a framed Georgia O'Keefe poster. I stopped to look more closely at a family portrait. Maxine was wearing a dress. It was very disconcerting to see her dressed that way. Plus I'd never pictured Maxine having a mother and a father—I thought she'd arrived fully grown, like Athena.

The phone rang. Maxine came into the living room to answer it. "Hello? Speaking. Well, I'm sorry you're in crisis but you're interrupting my dinner." She put the phone back in its charger.

"One of your students?" I asked.

"No," Maxine said. "A total stranger. Ever since *Lesbian Bed Death and Resurrection* was published, I keep getting these calls from lesbians who think I'm some kind of sex expert."

"Aren't you?" I asked.

"Et tu, B.D.," Maxine said.

"Is something burning?" Bridget asked.

"Shit! It's the bread." Maxine ran into the kitchen.

Bridget and I followed her. The crusts of the breads were charred and steaming. Bridget gave an especially loud sigh.

We sat down at the table and Maxine began ladling a brown, lumpy substance into the bowls in front of us.

"That looks incredible," Bridget said. "What is it?"

"Lentil soup."

I felt a twinge of anxiety. Was it lentil or barley soup that I didn't like? The first spoonful answered my question. I tried not to think about the mushy, pasty texture as I chewed and swallowed. My bowl seemed big enough to contain one of the Great Lakes.

Maxine brought a small cutting board that held what she had managed to salvage from the burnt loaves of bread. I snatched up two of the ragged, crustless slabs as soon as the board hit the table.

No sooner had I finished congratulating myself for making it through the soup when Maxine appeared with the main course.

"It's lasagna made from whole wheat pasta, spinach and tofu," she said, anticipating my question.

"Yum," said Bridget. "I love tofu, don't you, B.D.?"

I gave her what I thought was a glare worthy of Maxine.

"Oh!" Maxine said, jumping up from her chair. "I almost forgot the Brussels sprouts."

This wasn't supposed to happen to an adult. The everything-you-hate-to-eat meal was a child's nightmare. If I said I was allergic to Brussels sprouts, would Maxine believe me?

"Maxine, you've outdone yourself," Bridget said. "I can't imagine how you can possibly top this meal."

"I found this wonderful no-fat pistachio frozen yogurt."

I pressed my lips together and tried not to cry. I could deal with the nuts in Rocky Road and, if desperate, would tolerate butter pecan. But I loathed pistachio ice cream, and I considered frozen yogurt a crime against nature. "No thanks," I said. "The soup and the lasagna did it for me."

After dinner, Maxine showed me a couple of group pictures from her feminist commune days.

"You all have the same haircut," I observed.

"Yes, we cut each other's hair in the kitchen."

The hairstyle, if it could be called that, reminded me of a photograph of my father as a child. It looked as though someone had placed a bowl upside down on his head and cut around the edges.

"Where's your bathroom?" I asked.

"Through the kitchen, down the hallway, second door on the right," Maxine said. "Watch out for Paddington."

I was surprised that Maxine owned a teddy bear, much less kept it in her bathroom. I wondered why I had to watch out for it.

I opened the door, found the light switch and flicked it on, illuminating a very large snake coiled in the corner by the tile wall and the bathtub, within striking distance of the toilet. Slowly, I shut the light, backed out into the hallway, and closed the door.

"Did you find it?" Maxine called from the living room.

"Yes, I did," I called back. I stood in the hallway, trying to calculate how much time I had until I returned to my own apartment. Say another half-hour at Maxine's, maybe fifteen minutes to the subway, at least forty-five minutes to Manhattan if the trains were running frequently, an hour or more if they weren't, plus a five-minute walk to my apartment. Too long. I was trying to think if there was some place I could stop on the way home when Maxine came into the hallway.

"What's the matter, B.D.? Did Paddington spook you? He's harmless—I fed him today." She strode past me, opened the door, turned on the light, and bent down. The snake slithered up her arm and around her neck, and she carried him past me into the bedroom.

When I came out of the bathroom a second time, the bedroom door was closed.

Back in the living room, I asked Maxine, "Why do you have a snake and why is it called Paddington?"

"Oh, Paddington isn't mine; I'm just taking care of him for a friend."

—*mn*—

"Well, I think I should be on my way," Bridget said. "Can I drop you off at the subway, B.D.?"

"That would be great."

As I thanked Maxine for the wonderful dinner, she suddenly hugged me. It was so unexpected that I walked with Bridget to the car in a kind of shock.

"Maxine hugged me," I said. "Do you think that means she likes me? I don't mean 'like' like—you know, the girlfriend kind of like—more like she thinks it's OK that I exist in the same universe as she does."

"That dinner definitely had a deleterious effect on your brain," Bridget said.

"That was no dinner, that was assault and battery," I

said. I couldn't suppress a shudder as the soup, tofu lasagna, Brussel sprouts, and frozen yogurt reappeared before me as a kind of mental indigestion. "Maxine hugged me. Don't you find that amazing? She's never shown me any affection before."

"B.D., I don't understand why you're making such a fuss about a hug."

In the car I began taking a long-distance inventory of the contents of my refrigerator.

Bridget drove for a couple of blocks, then parked the car outside an old-fashioned diner.

"This isn't the subway," I said.

"No, but they make terrific ice cream sundaes in this diner. And ice cream sundaes don't require a lot of preparation time," Bridget said. "You have the air of a desperate woman, B.D."

"You know me so well."

Bridget ordered hot fudge with chocolate ice cream; I ordered butterscotch with vanilla.

"I have never been so glad to see a maraschino cherry in my entire life," I declared. I began working my way through the whipped cream, moaning softly.

Bridget laughed. "Are you coming or something?"

"No," I said. "This is better than sex."

Bridget looked concerned. "For your sake, I hope you're exaggerating."

I was halfway through the ice cream and sauce when the idea hit me. It was so perfect that I put my spoon down to contemplate it.

"Now what?" Bridget asked. "You look as if you're on the verge of speaking in tongues."

'I think I should host the next dinner," I said.

Bridget grinned. "And you're already planning the menu?"

"Yup," I resumed inhaling my ice cream. "Pâté to start," I said, spoon poised for re-entry. I paused to savor the ice cream and sauce before going on. "And none of that vegetable pâté either." I took another spoonful. "Maybe I'll do a baked Brie instead." My ice cream was approaching the soupy stage. "Then a filet roast. Baked potatoes with butter and sour cream. Asparagus with hollandaise sauce." I didn't really like asparagus, but I was willing to suffer for the sake of the sauce. The asparagus would be the price I'd pay for my revenge.

"And for dessert?" Bridget asked.

"Chocolate mousse cake with real whipped cream."

"And when are you going to have this dinner?"

"Well, I have to clean up my apartment first."

It was the fatal flaw in an otherwise brilliant plan. I recalled how Eduardo had once made the mistake of stopping by my apartment unannounced to drop something off. The instant he stepped through the door, he took out his newly acquired cell phone and called a friend, begging him to come and escort him home in a taxi, then brew him a tisane so he could recover from the shock.

Chapter 18

Angel and I were working our way through the top ten activities preferred by authors of personal ads. We had gone to a movie, visited a museum, and attended a play and a concert. We had traveled around the world via New York's ethnic restaurants, and had spent a day antiquing in a scenic village on the Hudson River. Angel had bought me a copy of *The House at Pooh Corner* to replace the one I'd given to my elementary school library because I felt guilty about an overdue book. We both disliked the blue M&Ms, and preferred the white icing to the chocolate on black and white cookies. Angel simply refused to eat the chocolate, while I ate it first and saved the best for last. And we had gone for walks in the park and on the now-empty beach with Betty Boop, Angel's Great Dane. At the end of each meeting, agreeing that it had been fun, we would stare at each other intently for a couple of minutes, then go our separate ways.

I was frustrated, but afraid of making the first move. However, I was getting a little tired of shopping for new lingerie every time Angel made a date with me.

Tonight, we were attempting a quiet evening at

home—Angel's home, of course, since mine was not in a state suitable for entertaining guests.

Angel proved to be a good cook. The meal she prepared was simple, but tasty—salad, roast chicken, wild rice, steamed vegetables, sorbet for dessert. After she served the coffee we settled in to watch *The Maltese Falcon*, one of Angel's favorite movies.

Angel put the DVD in and sat down in a recliner.

"There's plenty of room here on the sofa," I said.

Angel didn't take the bait. "I always sit in this chair when I watch DVDs."

Betty Boop jumped up and lay down next to me, with her head in my lap. I sighed.

When the movie was over, I started to shiver. I tried to control it, but when my teeth began to chatter, Angel looked at me.

"Are you cold?"

"Nnnnoooh," I said. It was hard to talk with my teeth making like the happy, tap-dancing feet in *42nd Street*. "This ha-happens whenever I tr-try to figure out if someone is going to m-make a p-p-p-pass at me. I can't t-t-t-take the suspense any longer. Either t-t-t-tell me that you just want to be friends, or k-k-k-kiss me."

She put me out of my misery without a word.

You might have thought I'd be engaged after that, but the voices in my head kept buzzing, fluttering, zapping themselves on the light. What if Angel wouldn't do the one thing I really needed her to do, the thing I was almost embarrassed about wanting because it was so identified with lesbians that my desire for it seemed boring and conventional? Maybe Angel was one of those women I'd read about who strapped on huge dildos and wanted them sucked. I tried to figure out why a woman would find this arousing. She wouldn't feel anything— unless it was a phenomenon like the phantom limb, but reversed. Or maybe it was a visual thing. When I came out of the closet, I thought I had left fellatio far behind, and I felt a bit resentful having it pop up again. Women's genitals were so much nicer; they were less ostentatious, and they never made you gag.

My internal disc jockey turned sadistic and began playing the refrain "Girls just want to have fun," like a taunt while the great storm cloud questions rolled slowly across my consciousness. *Am I going to cry? Will I be able to come?*

I had tried talking to Bridget about the crying, once. She shrugged and said that lots of women did, if that made me feel any better, which it didn't.

"Ticklish?" Angel asked, after my shoulders scrunched up in response to her nuzzling my neck.

"Yes. Sorry."

"I think we'll be more comfortable upstairs." She took my hand and led me up to her bedroom. Betty Boop was sprawled across the bed.

"Betty. Off the bed."

Betty yawned.

Angel picked up a rubber toy and squeaked it. Betty sat up, and then ran as Angel threw the toy out into the hallway.

I slid my hands under the sleeves of Angel's t-shirt and stroked her muscles. Then I slid my fingers down to her sides and under the cotton again, around and up to her shoulder blades, while I plucked at her upper, then lower lip with both of mine. We sank down onto the bed and everything shifted—weight and tempo and touch. There was a desperate quality to my need for both of us to be naked. I pulled my tank top off, and Angel put her hands behind my back.

"In front," I whispered.

I had to admit that I'd had some trouble with the clasp myself. Still, it was disconcerting to see a woman with a license to carry a .44 Magnum stymied by a bra that hooked in front.

Fortunately, I didn't have to face that problem because Angel wasn't wearing a bra. Beneath the white t-shirt her breasts formed soft, sweet peaks of meringue. I brushed the tip of one with the back of my hand.

"Do you mind?" Angel said. "I'm in the middle of a highly technical operation." A moment later she was able to slip the straps off my shoulders and hold the bra in the air. "We have lift off." She dropped it on the floor by the bed, and grasped the hem of her t-shirt.

I gasped and quivered.

"What?" said Angel, arms above her head, breasts exposed, the neck of the t-shirt stretching over the tip of her nose.

"Betty's licking my toes," I whispered. We both watched her for a moment.

"Would you like me to do that to you?" Angel asked.

I considered this. Perhaps if I'd had a pedicure, and was fresh from the bath, wearing that magenta silk robe I'd admired earlier in the week. "Actually," I said, wiggling my toes to dry them off, "I'd rather you lick something else."

Angel's eyes were the blue beginning of a flame. With her flushed cheeks and coppery hair, she was a creature of fire, an underworld goddess come to take me on a dark, heated journey. "The back of your knee?" she asked.

"An intriguing possibility, but not precisely what I had in mind."

"Your inner thigh?"

"I'd prefer that you bite that. But you're heading in the right direction."

Angel lay down on top of me, light in weight but solidly muscled. As our kisses became longer and deeper, our breathing shorter and more ragged, Angel began moaning, "B . . . B . . . B . . ."

That's one of the problems with having a name like mine—Bambi doesn't exactly fit into a Great Moments in the Heat of Passion scenario.

"B.D.," Angel sighed.

I held my breath while Angel's mouth moved up my inner thigh. As she lapped and circled and thrust, I offered up an inarticulate chant. But some part of my brain remained on guard duty. Was I making too much noise? Taking too long? I was afraid I might break if she kept on going. "Don't stop," I gasped, clutching the sheet with my hands. I wanted to be on overload, my clit so charged it would black out my brain like New York City in the summer of '77. But when I came it was less of a shattering than a slow sinking back into the here and now. I turned away from Angel, curled into myself, and wept.

"Are you OK?" Angel asked.

"I'm sorry," I said. "I don't understand why this happens; it just does."

"I don't mind," Angel replied, smoothing my hair. "I just want to be sure it's not because of something I did."

"You were wonderful," I said, and headed for the bathroom and a tissue. I decided that it wasn't the crying that was so bad, it was blowing my nose afterward.

From the doorway, I looked at Angel on the bed. Her patch of blonde pubic hair fascinated me and I lay down between her legs to take a closer look. Her hair was straighter, sparser, silkier than mine. I rubbed my face against her like a cat marking its territory, then turned back to lick her clean, alternating long slow strokes with quick flicks. With Angel's every moan, I became more predatory. When she pulled my head away, I lifted myself up and over. And then I, who had never been able to work a hula hoop, found my hips in orbit as I pressed myself to her.

With Angel curled behind me, her arm draped across my stomach, I listened to the nocturnal city sounds of the occasional car or subway train passing, and remembered Jean, my only woman before Angel. "You should make love with lots of women," she'd told me, and it wasn't so much an endorsement of promiscuity as an acknowledgment of pleasure taken and given, a kind of blessing. While my skin cooled and the scent of sex still lingered, I pictured myself lying on soft, shaded grass, entwined with an Amazon Bridget, then spreadeagled beneath the gaze of an imperturbable Maxine. But they were remote figures on my fantasy stage; it was a delightfully mortal Angel whose breasts caressed my back with every breath.

I was starting to doze when a new sound intruded. The snoring was impossible to ignore. I sighed, wondering if I'd ever get to sleep.

"It's not me," Angel said. "It's the dog."

I placed my hand over Angel's to hold her to me, and closed my eyes.

Chapter 19

"Look!" I said to Angel, holding up a purple silk camisole trimmed with café au lait lace. "It was on sale—reduced three times. I couldn't find the tap pants or slip that should go with it, though." I frowned. "I guess I'll just have to sort through my underpants for something."

"Why bother?" Angel said. "Just leave your bottom bare. In fact, why don't you wear those feathered stockings with it?"

I was shocked. "I can't wear those stockings with this camisole, Angel. They don't match."

"I promise not to notice, B.D. I'll have other things on my mind."

And so, on Halloween night, I dressed for Bridget's party in the purple silk camisole and the black feathered stockings, made decent by the nun's habit that I had rented again.

I'd been hoping that Angel might accompany me, so that I could finally introduce her to Bridget, Natalie, and Maxine. But Angel had yet another scheduling conflict. Dating a private investigator wasn't nearly as much fun as reading about one.

"But it's Halloween," I complained.

"My source is very paranoid. Halloween is the one day of the year when he feels it's safe to meet in person because so many people are wearing some kind of disguise."

As Angel drove me to Bridget's house, she kept touching the feathers circling my thighs with the tips of her fingers, as if to reassure herself that they were really there. With each touch, the fabric of my nun's robe stirred ever so slightly in response. I was sunk low in the seat with my knees drawn up in an attempt to keep from flattening the feathers on the underside of my thighs.

Angel stopped the car across the street from Bridget's house and leaned toward me, resting one arm behind my head. "Have a good time, sweetie," she whispered. I wriggled in my seat. When she kissed me, I expected her to pat the feathers one more time, but she surprised me with a caress that was equally delicate but directed between my thighs. The kiss ended with my panting a little and Angel saying, "I'll be waiting for you."

I had lost interest in the party at that point, but then I remembered that Angel had an appointment. "I won't be late," I said.

"B.D., this is Robin."

I recognized Robin immediately as the woman I had seen draping herself all over Bridget at the All-Girl Gala.

"Ohmygod. B.D.! I have heard sooooooooo much about you." The neck brace Robin was wearing detracted from her pirate's costume, but when I inquired about her accident, Robin said she always wore a neck brace at Bridget's to keep Alice B. from killing her by biting her jugular vein.

Alice B. was the smaller of Bridget's two cats. She had made what I thought was an eminently reasonable decision to devote one of her nine lives entirely to Bridget. Alice B. disdained the attentions of lesser beings, and could be quite vehement in her rejections.

"I can't see Alice B. committing murder," I said.

"Do you believe everything everyone tells you?" Bridget asked.

"B.D., you don't look anything like the way I pictured you," Robin said.

"Well, I don't usually appear as a nun."

"There seems to be a connection between lesbians and nuns," Robin observed. "Can you explain it?"

"Lots of passion, not much sex," Maxine interjected as she walked by with an empty bowl. It seemed an incongruous object for her to be carrying, for she was in leather from head to toe, bearing more chains than Marley's ghost.

"Nice costume, Max," Robin said.

"This isn't a costume." Maxine gave Robin a look that should have reduced her to road kill.

Maxine had deemed Robin's status within Bridget's crowd as "undecided," but according to Bridget, Robin had made no secret of her intent to make Bridget her first woman lover. Undeterred by Bridget's monogamy, Robin was operating on the theory that Bridget could be lured into the perfect bed. She spent her weekends testing mattresses, fingering sheets, and reviewing the ratings of and recommendations for down comforters in *Consumer Reports* Buying Guide. I admired her methodical approach, even though I couldn't very well support her objective, since it directly conflicted with mine.

I grabbed a handful of candy corn from a conveniently placed bowl and sat down in the chair next to it. I slunk down, resting my head on the curved wicker back of the chair, knees up, feet resting on the ottoman—my other reason for choosing that chair. I pictured the feathers drifting out beneath my habit like seaweed under water, and began munching the candy corn, contented as the proverbial cud-chewing cow.

"What's up, B.D.?" Bridget asked, taking the seat next to me.

"Natalie and Robin appear to be avoiding each other," I said.

Bridget sighed. "Natalie doesn't approve of Robin," she confided. "And Robin thinks she'd be a better girlfriend for me than Natalie."

Of course, I thought that I'd be a better girlfriend for Bridget than both Natalie and Robin combined, but I tried to appear disinterested. My nun outfit helped to lend credence to my detachment.

"The first time Natalie came to my house," Bridget said, "Gertrude, my big Siamese—"

"Fat Siamese," Natalie interjected, as she walked into the room.

"—jumped from the top of my bookcase, right onto Natalie's shoulder."

"And you thought it was funny," Natalie said.

"The expression on your face!" Bridget laughed. Then she said, "Hey, I gave you a nice massage to make up for it, didn't I?"

"I don't like cats," Natalie said. "They shed. And they smell. And they throw up."

"I'll probably end up as one of those old women with forty or fifty cats," I said.

"When I get old I'm going to eat cat food and spit on people," Bridget declared.

Natalie's expression made it clear that this was not

going to happen in her house or in her presence. "Maybe you'll take Bridget in as one of your cats," Natalie said. I thought she might be smirking at me. If she was, I wasn't offended. We all knew I'd take Bridget any time, on any terms.

Annalise and Ellen joined us. Ellen, wearing a Western shirt with fringe, informed me that she was Cay Rivvers from the movie *Desert Hearts*. Annalise, wearing a bathrobe, was Vivian Bell, the professor. "I'm not taking off my robe," she said.

"That's her favorite line," Ellen explained. "Is Angel here?"

"No," I said. "She had some P.I. business to attend to."

"I think you're making her up," Annalise said.

"She's real. In fact, she dropped me off here on her way to her meeting."

"What kind of a car does she drive?" Ellen asked.

"It has two doors and a sun roof and it's red—darker than a fire engine, but lighter than maroon. The license plate is, '694EVR.'" I got a little light-headed just thinking about it.

"What make is it?" Annalise asked. "What model? How much horsepower does it have?"

"I have no idea."

Annalise rolled her eyes. "You're such a femme."

Bridget laughed.

I placed my hands on my stomach in a contemplative pose and looked up at the ceiling, where a bare-breasted figure with wings and a mermaid tail flew above Bridget's head.

"What a beautiful angel," I said.

"It was a gift. I hate angels," Bridget said.

"A poet gave it to her," Natalie said to me, placing a large, fragrant bowl of freshly popped popcorn beside the smaller bowl of candy corn. I was in ecstasy.

"I remember the poet," Maxine said, gathering up

145

empty beer bottles. "She really had the hots for you, Bridget."

"You did get more goodies from her than from most of your other admirers," Natalie said.

Maxine laughed. "All you had to do was say, 'Gee, I've always wanted . . .' and she would get it for you."

"You could have done without the poems, though," said Natalie. "You were so embarrassed."

"Especially when Natalie quoted those poems to you in bed," Maxine added.

"Can I help it if women who are just coming out find me attractive?" Bridget said, I thought it seemed a bit like Fred Astaire wondering why any woman would want to dance with him.

In fact, I had also bought presents for Bridget—a couple of t-shirts and some books that I thought she would enjoy. I had given them believing I was special to her. Now I saw myself as one more figure in a long line of supplicants, bearing gifts. I shrank back into the cheap black fabric like a deflating soufflé.

"Does Robin give you things?" I asked Bridget.

"What did you say, B.D.?"

"I asked you if Robin gives you things."

"I guess so." Bridget looked around as if she wanted to change the subject or her location.

"You guess so!" Robin had walked in on the tag end our conversation. "Didn't I bring you flowers last night? Hmm?" She tousled Bridget's hair aggressively.

"Yes, you did."

"And?"

"And you gave me a vase to keep them in." Bridget leaned toward me and pointed to a small table against the far wall, where what had to be at least two dozen yellow, long-stemmed roses were guarded by Gertrude, Bridget's other cat. The Siamese had the ample body of her namesake, Gertrude Stein.

"My God! That's Baccarat crystal," I exclaimed.

Bridget looked quizzical. Robin looked impressed.

"I do bridal registries. I could run a *Jeopardy!* category on crystal, china, or silver." I knew that vase. It sold at retail for $800. Suddenly the books I'd given Bridget seemed pretty measly. They hadn't even been first editions, although one had been signed by the author.

"I'm going to get a beer," I said. "Anyone else want one? Bridget?" I wasn't really in the mood to wait on Bridget, but I have found courtesy to be a convenient screen for my emotions.

"Sure. Thanks, B.D." Bridget took an ice cube from an abandoned cup and pitched the cube toward Annalise's ample cleavage.

Annalise shrieked as the cube slid home. "I'm still not taking off my robe," she bellowed.

"Is it stuck? I'll get it, honey," Ellen said.

—*mm*—

As I walked back from the kitchen with a beer in each hand, I felt a quick poke between my buttocks. I would have jumped in any case, but since I wasn't wearing any underwear I felt especially vulnerable. I whirled around.

Robin giggled. "I just had to do that, B.D. I've always wanted to goose a nun." She scurried ahead of me and I watched as she whispered in Bridget's ear. Bridget looked at her and then at me, with a look I'd never seen on her face before. I knew then how the hundredth harem girl felt when the sheik finally got around to singling her out. Tonight was my night, but I was having none of it.

I handed Bridget one beer and put the other one on the end table, then turned and walked away.

147

"B.D.? Is something wrong?"

I didn't answer; I just kept walking toward the door. Bridget followed me all the way outside the house, then put her hands on my shoulders. "B.D., what is it? What's the matter?"

"Did Robin stay with you last night?"

"Yes. Sometimes she comes over, we order pizza and watch a couple of DVDs, and she spends the night."

"Do you make love with her?"

Bridget smiled, a secretive smile that I couldn't interpret. "She sleeps on the sofa. I told you, B.D., I'm monogamous."

"You've never asked me to sleep over your house." I heard the petulance in my voice and despised myself for it.

"We do other things together, B.D."

"Well, it's none of my business anyway." Dead leaves rattled as the wind pushed them along the cement, while voices only I could hear told me that I wasn't pretty enough, thin enough, smart enough, good enough. "Look," I said, "I really have to go. Angel's waiting for me."

"Hey! Not without a hug," Bridget said, making me feel like a child. Grudgingly, I uncrossed my arms, but I wasn't prepared for the way she scooped me up and mashed me to her—so hard my breasts hurt.

———

Slowly I walked on down the driveway by Angel's house, pausing to acknowledge the moon. "Hello, Goddess," I said. I could hear Betty Boop barking, heralding my return, and I knew Angel would be saying, "All right, Betty, all right, thank you for letting me know, now cool it." When I opened the door, Betty was calm and Sarah Vaughan was singing "Witchcraft." The music drew me up the steps to the bedroom, and I stopped short at the doorway. Angel had put black satin sheets on the bed and a vase of blood red chrysanthemums the size of grapefruits on the bureau. Votive candles glittered in the darkness like jewels in a treasure chest, and the air smelled of cinnamon. Angel was wearing black silk boxer shorts and a sheer black tank top. "You know what I want," she said.

I shed the nun's robe and left it puddled at my feet. It was only a couple of steps to the bed, but by the time I reached it, I felt as though I had forded a river and emerged cleansed.

Maybe it was all that candy corn, but I also felt fidgety. And although I knew perfectly well what Angel wanted, I wasn't sure I wanted to give it to her just yet. I pushed Angel down onto her back and straddled her legs. Then, with a little cooperation from her, I guided Angel's arms above her head, holding them there. She regarded me with surprise, amusement, and a little indulgence.

"Can I tie you up?"

"How thoughtful of you to ask," Angel said.

"Right over left, left over right, makes a knot neat, tidy and tight," I murmured, remembering the rhyme from my Girl Scout days.

"Ah, B.D.? You might not want to make the knot too tight."

"Good point, Angel."

"There are some Ace bandages in the medicine cabinet," Angel said.

The bandages appeared to be well used. "You've been tied up before, haven't you?" I asked, as I bound Angel's right hand to a handy spot on the headboard of her bed with the stretchy strip.

Angel nodded. She lifted her free hand and ran her thumb across my cheekbone, and her fingers along the

149

curve of my jaw. "But I have never had the pleasure of being tied up by a beautiful woman in feathered stockings."

I kissed her palm and the tip of each finger before wrapping her hand.

Once I had Angel in place, I regarded her briefly, then sighed.

"What?"

"Oh, I don't know. The sheets, the candles, the flowers—it's all so beautiful. These Ace bandages don't do anything for my esthetic sensibilities. I want to tie you up artistically, like a Japanese gift."

"Next time," Angel said.

I began by teasing and tickling her with the feathers. It was a little awkward, since they were part of the stockings on my legs, and at first I worried about what I must look like. But as Angel arched and twisted, gave little grunts and cries, I thought less about my limitations as a contortionist and more about what else I might do and how I might do it. I tried dragging the feathers across Angel's nipples and belly, then sweeping them up and down her body. Sometimes I followed the feathers with my lips, other times with my soft, wet cunt. I made Angel ask me three times to finish her off because, as I told her, three is a magical number.

After I untied her, Angel favored me with a slow, steady storm of feathery kisses over every inch of silk, then deep tongue kisses. Then she told me to close my eyes. I heard a drawer open and close, and it seemed like a very long time before I heard Angel say, "You can open your eyes now. And your legs, while you're at it." She moved toward me in the soft candlelight, the glitter in the dildo glimmering faintly as stardust.

"Angel!" I said. "I have one exactly like that."

She grinned; a wide, impish, jack-o-lantern grin.

In my mind I saw my child self at the top of a slide. I

sat down on the very top step, grasped the shiny metal sides, and held my breath. I slid slowly forward till my arms were stretched behind my back. And when I was ready, I pushed, let go, glided down.

Chapter 20

The invitation to Dana's annual New Year's Eve champagne potluck called for "BLACK attire." Since she was the owner of Basic Black, a boutique specializing in black clothing and household articles, I wasn't surprised.

When I showed the invitation to Angel, she said, "I've been meaning to talk with you about New Year's Eve, B.D."

"Oh, no. Angel, you can't, you absolutely cannot have any P.I. business on New Year's Eve."

"It's not business business, it's more like a convention."

"A convention? On New Year's Eve?"

"Maybe it's more like a retreat," Angel said.

"What are we talking about?"

"I'm going to be in San Francisco."

I just looked at her.

"Once a year I get together with a couple of dykes from the San Francisco Police Department and the Los Angeles Police Department, plus some West Coast-based P.I.s and a mystery writer."

"Wonderful, but why do you have to get together on New Year's Eve?"

"I don't know. We've never met on New Year's Eve be-fore. Someone suggested it, and we all thought it might be fun. I didn't even know you when we made the plan, B.D."

"I can't believe this," I said. "I've never had a date for New Year's Eve in my entire life, and now that I'm finally in a relationship my girlfriend is going to be out of town for the big night."

—*mm*—

I was convinced that I was going to die without ever having had a date for New Year's Eve. The more I thought about it, death seemed just around the corner. Every building façade was a potential killer, waiting to fling a brick down onto my head. And those sports utility vehicles that every self-respecting young urban profes-sional absolutely had to have to traverse the rough, potholed terrain from the Pottery Barn to the Apple store—I'd seen a *60 Minutes* segment on how unstable those monsters were. "There's a Range Rover waiting out there for me," I said to Angel. "And when it turns the corner and goes out of control and runs me over, you'll be sorry we didn't spend my last New Year's Eve on earth together."

"It'll probably be a Land Rover," Angel replied. "And if my plane crashes tomorrow, you'll be sorry you sent me off with so little affection."

"Y'know something?" I said. "You're right."

We didn't bother with the eleven o'clock news. At one point Angel rolled over, looked at the clock, and mumbled, "B.D., it's nearly two. I've got to get some sleep."

"Oh, but you're going to have that nice long plane ride tomorrow," I whispered. "You can sleep then."

"B.D., I really don't think I have the energy—"

I didn't let her finish. "Sweetheart, you don't have to do a thing. Just leave everything to me."

The alarm went off at 5:30. Even after a shower, Angel still looked a bit pale and frayed at the edges. She kissed me goodbye warily, as if she feared I might waylay her yet again and cause her to miss her plane. I had no such intention.

As she closed the front door, I saw it all so clearly: the slow wending through the long security line, the narrow coach seat, all of the space in the surrounding overhead bins already taken. Angel could be in the dreaded middle seat, and the person in front of her could put their seat all the way back. Then there would be the indignity of having to pay for a bottle of water, a sandwich, and a snack. Not to mention screaming infants, out of control children, and ill-tempered adults. The possibilities for a miserable travel experience were endless.

I scissored my legs beneath the sheet and redistributed the pillows. There are times when being single in a double bed is positively luxurious. I decided that after a couple more hours of well-earned sleep I would treat myself to breakfast at Dumpling, the local "comfort food" restaurant near Angel's house. Pancakes, perhaps, or scrambled eggs with crisp bacon, hash browns, and rye toast.

The day went so perfectly that I was sure there was a Goddess, and she was definitely a femme.

Breakfast was delicious. I softly hummed "Just you wait, 'enry 'iggins" while I drizzled maple syrup over the not-too-dark, not-too-light pancakes. The waitress was an utterly delectable gamine with shower-spiky black hair. I left her a very generous tip and headed for the subway to Manhattan and the stores on my mental list. They would be crowded, but there would also be after-Christmas sales.

I wanted a velvet dress. A kitten-soft, black velvet

dress that would tug at a hand to stroke it. And, in an all too rare conjunction of wish and fulfillment, I found it. No frills, just a lush cascade of black, flowing loosely out to float just above my knee.

—*mm*—

On my way out of the store, walking through the designer boutiques, I saw the shoes. They stood out on the sales rack like an Old Master in a room of Abstract Expressionists. The Parisian designer had updated the old-fashioned, lace-up ankle boot. The pointy toe, the lace-up flaps, and the three-inch stiletto heel were in black suede. The rest of the boot was a faux silvery lace on a charcoal fabric. I looked at the bottom of the shoe. $395—reduced to $249—reduced to $119—reduced to $59. And they were my size. I tried them on. They fit.

"A woman had these on reserve for months," the clerk told me as he rang up the sale. "When she finally decided she didn't want them, we had to mark them down several times. Plus, you get an additional twenty-five percent off anything you purchase with your store card today."

Desideratum, one of my favorite lingerie stores, was next. It was one of the shops on my trousseau tour, and I spent a fair amount of my own money there as well. So Kiko gave me a big hello.

"B.D.! I was thinking about you just the other day. Help yourself to some coffee."

I put down my bags and walked over to the little table with the coffeemaker, flowered sugar and creamer, mugs and real spoons.

"I need a pair of black stockings," I said.

"With or without seams?"

"I'm not sure." I showed Kiko my new shoes.

"Why not take a pair of each?" she said. "You can try

them on at home and decide which style looks best. You're sure to wear the other pair sooner or later."

"Sooner," I said. "That's a good idea. Now, do you have anything in a full slip that's my size?" I frequently complained to Kiko about the fact that so many of the bras I liked stopped at size 36. I had relegated small-minded lingerie designers to a special circle of Hell.

"That's why I was thinking about you," Kiko said. "I got a new shipment of slips in the other day, and put one aside for you. I was going to call, but of course, here you are." She went through the curtains into the back of the store and came back with a burgundy silk charmeuse full slip with black lace at the top and hem.

"Ooooh. Let me try it on."

In the dressing room, I adjusted the ribbon straps and breathed a sigh of relief, realizing I had room to do so. Hands on my hips, I twisted right, then left, watching myself in the mirror.

"How's it look?" Kiko asked.

"It's just what I want," I said.

That night I dreamed Bridget was pressing me into my bed, her hair tickling my cheek. I could have sworn I smelled her. I opened my eyes. As everything came into focus, I saw my cat on my chest and heard my phone ringing.

"Excuse me," I said to Truffle as I sat up and reached for the receiver.

"Hey, B.D., I didn't wake you, did I?"

"Angel, it's one o'clock in the morning."

"Is it? It's only ten o'clock here. I just thought you'd like to know that I arrived safely."

"I'm glad," I said. And I was.

"So, go back to sleep now."

"OK. Good night, Angel."

"B.D.?"

"Yes?"

"What are you wearing?"

I didn't reply right away. I was awash from neck to ankle in well-worn flannel. The cornflower blue background was fading to the white of the sheep, and the stars, once egg yolk yellow, were now the color of lemonade. The tiny buttons that closed the front of the gown had fallen prey to the washer one by one, and the slit on the left side, which originally ended at mid-calf, was now at my knee. "Just a little something I picked up today," I lied. "A satin nightshirt. I wish it were an inch or two longer, though—when I move around, it keeps sliding up over my hips."

There was a moment of silence. "Gee," Angel said, "I was sort of picturing you in an old flannel nightgown."

"I miss you," I said.

"I miss you too. Sweet dreams, sweetheart."

———

On the morning of New Year's Eve I was creaming butter and sugar in my grandmother's mixing bowl, the first step in my mother's chocolate cake recipe, when my buzzer rang. I leaned across the bureau where Truffle had been sleeping, pressed the "Talk" button, and asked, "Who is it?"

"WahWAHbabada." As usual, the response from the intercom was unintelligible.

I pressed the Door button and waited. I heard the elevator door open and the footsteps start off in the wrong direction, then turn back. When the bell rang, I looked through the peephole, saw a face, and opened the door, leaving the chain on.

"Special delivery from Buff Buds," said the blonde butch with a long box under her arm. She was wearing Doc Martens, black jeans, a black down jacket, and a black baseball cap with the Buff Buds logo: a rose

158

blooming from a fist, the arm flexed to show the bicep. Buff Buds was a flower shop in Chelsea. Eduardo and I used them occasionally; their tightly packed floral arrangements were popular with some of our clients. Other florists, however, spoke darkly about Don and Ron's choice of plant food.

As I signed the delivery slip, the butch said, "Glad to see you're getting some."

"Pardon?"

"Flowers."

"Oh," I said. "Actually, this is a first for me."

"Nice way to start the new year."

"Yes, it is. Happy new year."

"You too."

I placed the box on my bed, lifted the lid, and found a dozen long-stemmed red roses. The card read: "One for each hour the bells will chime/One for each kiss owed to Bambi Devine. Your Angel."

—*www*—

Dana opened the door wearing a garment worthy of the infamous enchantress Morgan Le Fay. It was not so much a dress as an accumulation of wisps.

A real fire was burning in the real fireplace. Votive candles lined the mantle, and a black and white portrait of Dana by a well-known lesbian photographer hung above it.

Bridget, Natalie, and Maxine were standing near the fireplace. Natalie was wearing harem-style black pants, the fabric sheer enough for me to just make out her thong, despite the fact that the lighting in Dana's apartment consisted of candles, candelabras, and wall sconces, bolstered by one lamp with a 60-watt bulb. A scoop-necked camisole stopped just short of Natalie's midriff. Even without the spaghetti straps, it would have been obvious that she wasn't wearing a bra. Bridget watched her, and the reactions of the other women to her, with obvious enjoyment.

Bridget was decked out in black jeans, a white cotton shirt with the top button undone, and a loosely knotted black tie. I noticed that she also had on her down-at-the-heel, scuffed toe, unpolished black boots. For some reason I had yet to fathom, those boots always made me yearn to slither up her body, despite my being more elephant than eel.

Maxine had on black leather pants and a black brocade vest. As she reached across a side table for a glass of red wine, I noticed that she too was not wearing a bra. I decided to check out the small terrace, just off the bedroom. Bridget followed me out. "You're all gussied up tonight, B.D."

I was wearing the burgundy silk slip under my new black velvet dress, and I had decided to wear the seamed stockings with the silver, faux lace boots.

"Are you wearing real stockings?" Bridget asked.

"Is it more fun for you to know or for you to guess?"

Bridget chuckled the way a lioness might—a low, rumbling sound that I felt at the base of my spine. "Why, B.D., I believe you're dangerous."

"I'm glad to see you appreciate it," I said. "And you didn't answer my question."

"I'd rather guess."

"Then I plead the fifth," I said, and we walked back to the party.

Natalie was inspecting the buffet. In true potluck spirit, the offerings on the table ranged from caviar to comfort food. I watched Bridget reach for a serving spoon that was standing at attention in the middle of a macaroni and cheese casserole. "No," Natalie said. If she'd had a leash, she would have jerked it. "You can eat Maxine's salad."

I took a little bit of everything except the caviar, and a heaping portion of the macaroni and cheese. Then I wandered over to the window seat which looked out on Lower Manhattan and the Brooklyn Bridge. A moment later, Bridget was standing beside me, her back to the room and to Natalie. I lifted up my plate and she dipped her fork into the Velveeta-y mass. That's the kind of girl I am. Subversive.

After she finished the macaroni and cheese, Bridget went to get us both more wine. As she handed me my glass, she sat down on the opposite end of the window seat. The night was clear and the bridge glowed in front of us, but we were looking into each other's eyes.

If you want to imagine Bridget's eyes, go to a museum, one that has Monet's paintings of the water lilies in the gardens at Giverny. When you find a painting, or if you are lucky, more than one, take a seat—there is sure to be one in the gallery. Take in the greens the way you would soak up sun. The greens of the willows, sun-sheathed and shaded, of the reeds, of the Japanese bridge over the water strewn with lily pads and flowers. As you breathe in this universe of green, let yourself feel that you've been here before. And listen carefully to hear yourself singing in exquisite harmony with one other singer in the great life chorus. This sort of connection was what made Bridget my obsession.

I could never tell Bridget any of this, of course. I knew better than to speak about matters of the soul with a jovial butch jock.

Natalie came over to compliment me on my chocolate cake. I told her it was an old family recipe, taking a perverse pleasure in the knowledge that the secret ingredient was an entire can of Hershey's chocolate syrup.

The whole party trooped up to the roof to watch the

fireworks, along with groups from other apartments in Dana's building.

Natalie and Maxine stood at the stone balustrade; Bridget and I stood behind them. Bridget tried to slip her hands inside the open front of Natalie's leather coat, but Natalie slapped them away. "Your hands are cold."

"I know. I wanted to warm them on you."

"Put them in your pockets."

At the first peal of the bells, Natalie checked her Rolex. "It's twelve o'clock," she declared. "Everyone has to kiss the person standing next to them." None of us did.

I could have told Natalie that it wouldn't work. You can't trick people into kissing you. I had tried back in high school, when I invited Jerry Greenblatt to a holiday party and from the hallway light, hung a sign that said: *This isn't mistletoe, but you can kiss me anyway.* When Jerry walked through the front door he read the sign, laughed—and kissed my hand.

So Maxine stared out at the brilliant colors punctuating the night sky while Bridget and Natalie exchanged a perfunctory kiss. I didn't want to impose my lips on Bridget's; I wanted her to kiss me on her own terms.

I thought of Angel, then remembered that Bridget had kissed me once—the first time I gave her a t-shirt for no reason except my feeling that she would like it. It was the night she told me she was monogamous. And, in fact, there was nothing about the kiss that was disloyal to Natalie. It was a solemn event, shy and fleeting.

"I'm cold," Natalie said. "Let's go." Maxine turned and began walking with Natalie, joining the exodus from the rooftop.

Bridget touched the sleeve of my coat. "Let's hang out here for a minute. There are way too many people for those tiny elevators." Then, as she led me away from the balustrade, she asked, "Shall we dance?"

It wasn't exactly intimate: wool coat to wool coat. Our cheeks were chilled at the first touch, but they quickly thawed into a patch of warmth. We danced in silence, without words or music. And I thought that if it was true that your life passed before you when you died, I wanted to revisit this moment.

Bridget was the first to move her head, permit her lips to drift across my cheek. I followed her, my lips setting a path of their own. Our mouths were slightly open in anticipation of meeting. The tip of her tongue touched mine, gently as a snowflake, and a shooting star fell through my body, rushing out between my legs in a Niagara of heat. I swayed a little as I stepped back from her, into the silence. Bridget noticed and smiled— a pensive echo of her usual beam. Then she turned toward the door and I followed her lead once again.

Chapter 21

Passion Flower had only twelve tables, each accommo-
dating just two people, so reservations for the restaurant
had to be made at least three months in advance. Small
lamps fringed with pink silk shades provided soft, flattering light and orchids spilled across the milky damask
tablecloths. Framed erotic drawings, prints, and photographs of women together hung on the walls.

I had had some concern about my three-inch crimson
heels, but Angel was wearing her cowboy boots, so the difference in our heights was not that much more than usual.

Angel touched her wineglass to mine. "To the debut
of my thigh harness." My heart raced and I felt some
moisture and pulsing farther down. I would have run my
foot up her leg, but my shoes had straps and I
couldn't slip them off.

A few weeks earlier, Angel and I had marked up a
Good Vibrations mail order catalog. I used a pink felt tip
pen; Angel used purple. We both put a check next to the
Chocolate Mocha Love Crème, which I was now carrying
in my purse. In *Gentlemen Prefer Blondes*, Marilyn
Monroe as Lorelei Lee loves finding new places to wear
diamonds. I love finding new ways to eat chocolate.

Dessert is the first thing I look at on a menu. In my family we always had at least three or four dessert choices at holiday gatherings, because those who were supposed to bring an appetizer or side dish almost always brought dessert as well. Passion Flower's menu boasted of having "the best tiramisu on the East Coast." I thought perhaps I'd save the love crème for another night.

"Did you hear that Celeste and Francine broke up?" Angel asked.

"Yes," I said. "In fact, I saw Celeste last week. She looked—fantastic." I felt a little guilty acknowledging this.

Angel was nodding her head. She had a cynical yet sage expression on her face.

"Celeste has a whole new image," I said. "Before, she was a bit . . ."

"Dowdy?" Angel suggested.

"Well, yes. But now she's a really snappy dresser. She was practically swaggering down the sidewalk when I saw her."

Angel began to expound on one of her favorite theories—lesbian couples stayed together, no matter how unhappy or bored they might be, because the prospect of dating seemed worse. In her opinion, almost no one was having sex.

But if Angel saw the glass as half empty, I saw it as overflowing. I was convinced that everyone was having sex all the time.

I told Angel that she should run her theory by Maxine. Maybe it was my thinking of her, but I suddenly realized that Natalie and Maxine were seated at a table in the opposite corner of the room.

Natalie, having inhaled and swirled, had apparently decided to reject the wine. The wine steward was an imposing woman—tall, intricately tattooed, and blatantly packing, but I knew that she had met her match in terms of *hauteur*.

"I see Natalie and Maxine," I said.

"So?"

"Well, I just wouldn't have expected to see them here—together."

Angel directed a professionally surreptitious glance toward Natalie and Maxine, turned to me, and gently placed her hand on mine. "I worry about you," she said. "You've been speculating about their relationship for as long as I've known you. This should confirm your suspicions. Believe me, those two are together."

"How can you tell?"

"I see this kind of thing all the time in my investigations," Angel said. "That kind of knowledge comes with the territory."

I thought of Bridget, who was at a meeting of the International Society of Hosiery Makers in Paris, Texas. I'd asked her to bring me a pair of stockings.

Then, Angel whispered the name she growls into my ear in the dark, and she had my full attention.

—*mm*—

Angel slid the velvet dress up and off me. Standing in my silk leopard print slip, black lace garter belt, and stockings, I experienced the familiar fear of being found ridiculous.

"What?" Angel asked, but she kissed me before I could answer.

Later, while we were getting our second wind for the second time, I told Angel that Natalie had put Bridget on a very strict diet, and that Ellen and Annalise had speculated that there was a sexual reason.

"I like a woman to have some padding," Angel said, settling into mine. "Bone rubbing bone is no good."

167

Chapter 22

I squeezed fresh oranges using my grandfather's Sunkist juicer and made French toast with lots of cinnamon because Angel loved it that way. I served the French toast with sliced strawberries and bananas, and even warmed the real maple syrup.

I let Angel make the coffee because she was particular about it, and I'm not, so long as it has caffeine.

After breakfast, we took a shower together. I don't know if we actually saved any water or spent more time soaping and stroking than if we'd done it separately, but as it turned out, in planning for Pride Sunday, Angel had allocated for the time spent, if not the water. We had plenty of time to dress before making our way down to the Village to watch the parade.

I put on a faded lavender t-shirt with a snarling wildcat emblazoned in black across the front.

"Where'd you get that?" Angel asked.

"My first lover sent it to me after she returned home to London," I replied. "She told me I was fierce."

Angel smiled. "You are."

"Have you ever wanted to ride a motorcycle?" I asked Angel as the Sirens roared by.

"No," she replied. "But I do have a leather jacket."

"I'll settle for that," I said. I've always preferred the merry-go-round to the roller coaster anyway. "Will you wear it with a white, ribbed-cotton undershirt?"

"If you'll wear one of those old-fashioned, white nightgowns."

"With long sleeves and lots of little buttons and a high neck that ties with a ribbon?" I asked.

"Uh-huh."

"Oooh, am I a good girl?"

"You are," Angel said. "But secretly you want to be very bad."

"So you're going to do me the favor of taking me to some den of iniquity and doing terrible things to me?" I asked happily.

"That's right," Angel said. "And you are going to be very, very grateful."

I could hardly wait.

m~

Eduardo had planned to march with the Gay Men, Lesbians, Bisexuals, and Transgender People of all Colors and Classes United to Fight the Right for the Right to Marry wearing bridal regalia, but the organization had had some PR concerns.

"They said to me, 'Eduardo, you know that the TV people are going to photograph you, you'll be representing the gay marriage movement on the local news, you may even end up in some propaganda film that will be shown to church groups. All the straight people will point at you and scream, *See, that's what we're going to get*, and the athletes and actors will all stay in their closets because they don't want to be identified with you. Please, Eduardo, couldn't you just wear a white polo shirt like the rest of us?'"

"Do you know your queer history, honey?" Eduardo asked me. "It was the drag queens that started Stonewall, not some little button-down boys quibbling over who's going to sit at what table."

So Eduardo marched with four of his friends, all dressed up as bridesmaids, keeping a discreet distance from the official group. They opted for a Southern belle theme, and Eduardo looked very fetching in his off-the-shoulder, hoop-skirted bridal gown. He carried a sign that read: Gay Marriage Today, Not Tomorrow at Tara. I was proud of him. I felt that any man who walked over fifty blocks in high heels was a better woman than I was.

An older cop, showing signs of stoicism and sunburn, stood by as one of Eduardo's bridesmaids tossed his bouquet to a younger cop who was more likely to be voted one of New York City's finest. The officer caught the flowers in an impressive display of reflex reaction, and to the delight of the crowd, tipped his cap at the bridesmaid. A product of sensitivity training—or perhaps a future member of the Gay Officers Action League.

Stepping in time to the beat of the drums, a baton twirler—a slim proud figure a bit apart from the mass of band behind him—tossed his silver wand into the bright summer air. I followed it to the apex of its flight, two or three stories above the street, and back down again to where it landed, firmly, in his waiting hand. The whistles and cheers soared up and around as the baton twirler moved on. Had he wanted to twirl in high school? His high school's loss is our gain, I thought. Some good comes from dreams deferred.

The cheers of the crowd increased in volume as the

Parents and Friends of Lesbians and Gays marched by. A woman who was wearing a I Love My Lesbian Daughter t-shirt, opened her arms as if she would embrace us all, and my eyes filled with tears. I knew my parents loved me, but it was one thing for them to tell me, and quite another to proclaim it to the world.

I called out to Maxine as she walked by with Lesbians Out in Academic Environments, and she broke away from the group and came running over to me. "I'm collecting kisses from women-born-women wearing lipstick," Maxine said, turning her head from side to side to display her collection. "My lips are off-limits, though," she warned.

"Would you mind?" I asked Angel.

"I guess not," she replied. "It's an interesting approach to body art."

I handed Angel my hat and sunglasses to hold, and spreading the collar of Maxine's denim shirt, bent my head, aiming for the delicate hollow at the base of her throat. In preparation for landing, I wet my lips and parted them slightly. I hovered for a moment, then lightly pressed my lips to the spot, dabbing the salt of her sweat with the tip of my tongue. When I pulled away, my lipstick, Manic Panic's Sacrifice, had left a noticeable impression, but Maxine seemed unaffected by the experience.

Annalise, who never wore lipstick and had no use for rules, bounded up out of nowhere and gave Maxine a huge kiss on her off-limit lips.

"Hey!" Maxine yelled. "I didn't consent to that."

"So sue me," Annalise said. "The lesbian and gay lawyers are right behind you."

I turned to take my hat and sunglasses back from Angel. "I hope your lips aren't off-limits," I said.

"Not to you," she replied.

Ellen and Annalise had invited me to an after-the-parade party at their house. Angel had some computer work to do on a missing person case, so I went by myself.

Natalie lounged on a cushioned lawn chaise like an odalisque, while Maxine sat on the grass beside her, looking as if she should be cooling her with a feathered fan. Lacking one, she was amusing herself by tying some of the helium balloons to Natalie's ankles and wrists.

Natalie told me she had watched the parade from a lounge chair on the sidewalk.

"Didn't people try to stand in front of you?" I asked.

"I invited a friend with two Dobermans to watch with me," Natalie said. "We had plenty of room."

Meanwhile, Bridget and Gayle, who had come from New Jersey for the Pride celebrations, were shaking hands. Actually, they were not so much shaking as gripping, in a way that made me think of John Wayne. "What's with those two?" I asked Annalise.

She tsked and made an impatient gesture with her hand. "Oh, back in the Ice Age Bridget beat Gayle at arm wrestling, or Gayle went home with some femme Bridget had her eye on, or some such nonsense."

Eventually they both let go and Bridget bounced onto the wicker settee next to Gayle's lover, Hannah. The grin on Bridget's face approached a leer, and Hannah was a woman on the verge of a simper. Bridget put her arm across the back of the settee as Hannah turned her body toward her. "So, Bridget, I want to hear all about your latest conference."

"I'm going to be motivating the National Society of Cereal Chemists," Bridget said. "In Vienna."

"Vienna! How exciting!"

173

"Actually, it's the one in Illinois."

"What?"

"Vienna, Illinois," Bridget said.

"Oh, Bridget, you're such a tease."

"Well," Gayle said, "I'll just leave you two alone now." She strode over to the grill, where she flipped the hamburgers with more vehemence than skill.

I settled into an old webbed aluminum frame recliner and regarded the cloudless sky through a leafy veil. I had a paper plate with just-made guacamole and sun-warmed chips on my lap, and I held a frozen strawberry daiquiri in my right hand. I took a sip, swishing the delightful slush around in my mouth, and wondered what my cousin Sarah and her partner, Cathy, were doing in Berkley. My cousin David and his partner, Phillip, were either hosting a party or going to one. I tried to remember if London's Pride celebration was the same date as New York City's. Was Jean still dating the woman she'd mentioned in her last letter, three months ago? I watched sunlight spill over Bridget's hair and imagined her face a kiss away from mine. I swallowed the last of the daiquiri and closed my eyes.

When I opened them, Bridget was bending over me, refilling my glass, and Natalie was mouthing words at me. I couldn't figure out what she was trying to convey.

Natalie rose from her chair, sauntered over to Bridget, and put her lips very close to Bridget's ear. Suddenly Bridget shimmied back three feet or so. "Nasty girl," she murmured, "blowing in my ear." Natalie looked at me significantly.

I was more confused than ever. Had Natalie been trying to tell me to blow in Bridget's ear? Why would she do that? Or was she just trying to impress me with her technique?

Bridget returned with the daiquiri pitcher and began

making the rounds once more. "May I top you?" she asked me.

"Please." I held up my glass.

Maxine frowned. "I think you've had enough, B.D."

I had had a vision that I was eager to share. "I know what you should do for next year's parade, Natalie," I said. "You should have Bridget and Maxine carry you in one of those things."

"What are you talking about?" Natalie demanded.

"It's like a stretcher," I said, "except that instead of a piece of cloth there's a sort of throne with a canopy. You could wear something golden and shimmery. The throne and canopy could be red and purple or purple and red, and the poles could be wound with ribbons in the colors of the rainbow flag. Bridget and Natalie could wear loose pants and vests and little embroidered hats and trot down Fifth Avenue with you in-between."

Natalie was not amused, but Bridget was laughing. "Are you wasted, bambino?" she asked, ruffling my hair. I butted her hand the way a dog does when it wants you to keep petting it.

Gayle and Hannah were talking about people they'd seen that day—old friends, former rivals, exes and enemies. I thought I recognized one of the names as that of a locally prominent grassroots organizer.

"I had sex with her in a bathroom one time," Annalise said.

Ellen looked shocked, and a little jealous.

"It was long before I met you, honey," Annalise told her. "I was bad when I was young."

"I was bad too," Bridget said.

"You were the worst," Annalise replied.

Why couldn't I have known Bridget then, I wondered. I might have had a chance for a night with her. I raised my glass and said solemnly, "Timing is everything, isn't it?"

"Are you OK?" Bridget asked me.

"I was just thinking about all the years I wasted, not knowing who I was," I said. "I can never get them back."

"Do you have any regrets?" Bridget asked Maxine.

"None whatsoever," she replied in a self-satisfied tone.

Bridget turned to Natalie. "What about you? Any regrets?"

"Yes," Natalie said. "You."

I started to cry.

"It's OK," Bridget said, turning back to me. "I'm used to it."

Maxine lit into Bridget. "Why did you give B.D. all those drinks? You know she has a very low tolerance for alcohol."

Bridget affected the innocent surprise of a cat that has inadvertently knocked an invaluable *objet d'art* onto the floor.

"I hope she doesn't throw up," Natalie said.

"Are you getting your period?" Annalise asked me.

"I'll drive B.D. home," Bridget said.

Natalie stared at her a moment. "Fine. I'll be at Maxine's."

"Bitch," Bridget said, ever so softy.

———

In the car, I started to cry again—a slow-motion procession of single tears. "If you were my girlfriend," I said, "I'd let you eat whatever you wanted. I'd tell you every day that you're the most wonderful woman in the world."

"B.D.—" Bridget began, I interrupted her. "I'd take you to Paris, France."

"It's just a crush, B.D.," Bridget said. "Let it go. You've got Angel now."

I hate the word "crush." It's like being told that some treasure, imbued with emotion and history because it's been in your family for generations, isn't worth jack shit in the real world.

"Angel's my lover," I said. "But you're—my soul mate."

"B.D., I'm not the woman you're making me out to be."

"Maybe you're just not seeing yourself clearly. Or if I am mesmerized by an illusion, maybe I'm not the only one."

"What the hell is that supposed to mean?"

"Is it worth it? Is whatever you get from Natalie worth the constant chipping away at you?"

"Well, obviously it must be."

"Fine," I said as the car slowed down in front of my apartment building. "As your friend, I just want you to be happy. If it makes you happy to have Natalie slice and dice you, then I guess my role is to offer you the novelty of kindness."

I got out of the car.

"Don't slam the door, B.D.," Bridget warned.

"I know—your car is fragile, but your ego isn't. You can fucking close the door yourself, Bridget."

As I stomped up the steps to my apartment building, I felt the thud of the car door closing and heard the tires sigh as Bridget drove away.

Chapter 23

My emotional hangover was worse than the one from the alcohol. I dreaded going into work, for Eduardo was as adept at extracting intimate details from me as a gourmand at prying a juicy escargot from its shell. He never scheduled clients for the day after Pride Sunday, so there was no question of hiding behind my professional demeanor.

When I walked in the door, Eduardo took one look at my face and came toward me like an undertaker greeting the next of kin.

"*¿Que pasa, bebé?*"

I didn't even try to put up a front. "I had a fight with Bridget."

"What about? No, wait—go out to our little garden, sit down, relax, and I'll bring you some breakfast."

"I'm not hungry," I said.

"Oh, please, B.D. Now how about some music? What are you in the mood for?"

"Mozart's *Requiem.*"

Eduardo put his hands on his hips and regarded me over the top of his glasses. "B.D., who is *la loca* in this office?"

"You are, Eduardo."

He turned and walked toward the CD player. A moment later, Judy Garland was singing "*On the Sunny Side of the Street.*"

When Eduardo joined me in the garden, he was accompanied by André from the bakery around the corner. He was carrying a tray with two bowls of café au lait and freshly baked croissants and *pain au chocolates.*

"The ultimate in decadence," Eduardo declared. "Having your breakfast delivered."

"Thank you, André," I said. "I hope this wasn't too much trouble."

"Not at all," André said. "And if the *pain au chocolat* does not heal your heart, stop by this afternoon—I'm making éclairs."

"Now," said Eduardo, sitting down at the small, round cast-iron table, "tell me. What happened?"

I recapped the scene at the party, and then the one in the car.

Eduardo shook his head. "A classic mistake, B.D. Never take sides. Leave loyalty to Lassie."

I called Bridget from the office, and got her answering machine. The following day she left a message on my voicemail. When I called her back, she picked up.

"The third time is a charm," she said.

"I'm sorry. I was out of line."

"Apology accepted," Bridget said. "Want to have dinner?"

———

When we met again, it was as though we were in a newly whitewashed room; both of us were being careful not to do anything that might mar the pristine surface. We talked about books and movies, nothing personal—until the end.

180

"I really like hanging out with you, B.D.," Bridget said. "I want us to be friends. Please. I know how this is going to sound, but I really don't need another woman with a crush on me. I need a friend."

I could tell that Bridget was speaking from her heart. But in order to give her the response she was hoping for, I couldn't speak from mine. "I want us to be friends too," I said.

Of course, I still wanted much more than that. But if it were an all-or-nothing choice, I'd settle for having Bridget as a friend over not having Bridget in my life at all.

Chapter 24

I was watching *An American in Paris*. Gene Kelly and Georges Guétary sat at a small, round café table, waxing eloquently about love, while Oscar Levant sat between them, gulping coffee, calling for brandy, and fumbling with cigarettes—because he knew that Gene and Georges were in love with the same woman, and on the verge of finding that out.

As the first strains of "'S Wonderful" filled the room, Angel said, "Look at them—dancing in the street with complete disregard for traffic. B.D., I don't understand how you can watch these things."

"Sssshhh!" If I were watching the movie with Bridget, she'd probably be singing along. At least she loved a Gershwin tune.

Thinking of Bridget inspired me to create a lesbian subtext for the film. Muscular Gene Kelly was Bridget, while Leslie Caron was a kinder, gentler Natalie, waiting in the wings. Georges, exuding joie de vivre, represented Maxine, though I'd never describe her as joyful. Once I had heard Maxine tell Bridget that she could match her lyric for lyric, any day—she just didn't choose to do so. And of course I was Oscar Levant, waiting and dreading the inevitable collision of people and emotions.

By the end of the movie, all of Oscar's fears have come to naught; Gene Kelly and Leslie Caron wind up together.

But the following night, Annalise phoned to tell me that Bridget was in the hospital.

"What happened?" I asked.

Angel looked up from the book she was reading.

"Mushroom poisoning," Annalise said.

"Mushroom poisoning?"

"You know Bridget had a football party last weekend."

"No, she didn't invite me."

"Well, it was a football party, B.D. Anyway, Natalie made pizza with wild mushrooms. I have to say, that pizza was really delicious."

"But the party was four days ago," I said. "When did Bridget get sick? When did she go to the hospital?"

"There are lots of poisonous mushrooms, B.D. Maxine said the doctor explained that Bridget must have eaten one of the really bad ones—the fatality rate is something like fifty percent."

"Oh, please, don't say that," I said.

"The doctor said it was already too late when her symptoms showed up. There's no antidote. It doesn't look good. Bridget probably won't make it."

"What about the other people? My god, Annalise, you ate the mushroom pizza too!"

"That's what's so weird, B.D.," Annalise said. "There were about ten of us. But no one else got sick. Bridget was the only one."

I put the phone down as though it were made of glass.

"Bridget's in the hospital with mushroom poisoning," I said to Angel. "Annalise said she's probably going to die."

"Is there anything I can do?" Angel asked.

"Hold me," I said.

"Sure." She cradled me, gently stroking my hair.

"Bridget's strong," I said. "Maybe she'll make it through this."

"Maybe," Angel replied.

When Angel went to bed, I turned out the lights and curled up on the sofa, hugging one of the small pillows to my chest. I remembered the fight I'd had with Bridget after the Pride party, and our subsequent reconciliation. Though we'd agreed that we wanted to be friends, I had found it difficult to keep up my end of the bargain. We never talked about it, but I think Bridget suspected that my feelings for her hadn't really changed.

Later that night, with Angel's arms around me, I lay waiting for tears but none came. Despite Angel's physical presence, I felt alone.

In the dark, something wet touched my hand. Betty Boop had come to keep me company. She licked my hand several times and then I stroked her head and neck. I thought of Bridget's cats, Gertrude and Alice B. I wondered who was taking care of them.

The next day, I stayed in Angel's house, reading without comprehending, watching television, making lists of things I needed to do for work, while I tried not to think about the phone call I was dreading. It came around nine o'clock; Annalise told me that Bridget was gone.

I sat in the dark on a chair in the living room for most of the night, remembering the good times and the bad times I'd had with Bridget. I wondered if she'd known she was dying, and if she'd been afraid. I realized that the only picture I had of her was the one I'd cut out from the paper. In the morning I called Annalise to ask if she knew what was happening with Bridget's cats.

"I think Dana's taking care of them for the time being," Annalise said. "She usually looked after them whenever Bridget was away."

But would Dana want to take care of them permanently? I knew Natalie didn't like cats, and I suspected that Maxine wasn't all that fond of them herself. I called Natalie's number. Maxine answered the phone.

"How's Natalie doing?" I asked, after I had expressed my shock and condolences.

"Natalie's a very private person," Maxine said. "Even though she seems to be okay, I'm sure she's hiding a lot of what she's feeling."

"I understand," I said. "Look, do you know what's happening with Bridget's cats?"

"Dana's taking care of them," Maxine said. "But we need to find them a new home."

"I'll take them," I said.

I hadn't been in Bridget's home since the Halloween party, almost a year ago. It felt wrong, being there without her. Natalie and Maxine were putting Bridget's clothes into bags to take to the thrift shop, at her mother's request, when I arrived to pick up the cats.

I surprised myself by asking if I could have one of the shirts. "One of the flannel ones," I said. "It might comfort the cats in the new space, to have something with her smell on it."

"Then you should take one of the ones we were going to wash before giving it away," Maxine said, rummaging through one of the bags. She handed me a rumpled shirt.

Alice B. came into the room, yowling. It was a plaintive, piercing sound, almost as though she was asking, "Why?" Tears welled in my eyes; I brushed at them with my fingertips, smearing them over my cheeks.

"Shut up already," Natalie mumbled. She saw me looking at her, and seemed to realize how uncaring she sounded. "Alice B.'s been doing that the entire time we've been here. It's getting on my nerves," she said to me.

I found the cat carriers, set them on the floor and

opened them. Alice B. walked right into one and lay down. Gertrude was much more recalcitrant.

Truffle wasn't too pleased about what he considered to be intruders into his territory, but after a few initial spats, the three of them settled down, and at night my bed got pretty crowded. Truffle liked to lie against my left side, his head on my arm; Gertrude curled up at my feet. Alice B. would lie on my chest until I fell asleep; then she moved to my pillow.

As it turned out, neither Gertrude nor Alice B. was interested in Bridget's flannel shirt. When they first arrived I left it spread out on my bed, but they didn't go near it, and at the end of the day I hung it in my closet.

The following night, I held the shirt in my hands, pressed it to my face and smelled it; rubbed my cheeks against it. Then I slipped each arm into a sleeve, as reverently as a priest putting on vestments. I wrapped my arms around myself, sank down into a chair, and finally cried.

Chapter 25

I hated funerals. I hated clerics intoning false intimacies from notes jotted down on an index card. I hated open coffins displaying the discarded carapace of the body, irrefutable evidence that the soul animating self has seeped away.

So I was relieved when Natalie told me Bridget's family had agreed to cremation, which Bridget had specified in her will, and a memorial service a month after her death.

Angel insisted on accompanying me to the latter. "You've talked about Bridget so often, B.D., I feel like I knew her."

I didn't have much contact with Natalie or Maxine in the month that had passed. Maxine had called me, once, to ask how the cats were adjusting, and Natalie had offered to give me the angel I had admired at the Halloween party. "I think Bridget would like for you to have it, B.D."

I was glad to see that Maxine, not Natalie, was going to give the eulogy. In all the time I'd known them, I'd never heard Natalie say anything nice about Bridget in public.

Bridget's memorial service wasn't much different from any other New York City lesbian gathering—almost every woman there wore black. The outfit of choice seemed to be a black pantsuit with a tailored shirt, but a few women wore plain black dresses.

Natalie was all in black, right down to her pearls. A simple silk blouse, sheer enough for allure, yet without even a hint of the slutty, and wool crepe pants with a crease that didn't quit.

I wondered if she'd had the pearls all along, or if she'd zipped into Tiffany the morning of the memorial service.

But Maxine was all in white—pants, shirt, and vest. Despite being drenched in the color of purity, she still gave the impression that the devil had come a courtin'. Someone must have remarked upon her choice of color, for I overheard Maxine say, with her typical asperity, "White is the color of mourning in the Shinto religion."

"Oh, are you into that now?"

"My spirituality is not limited to a particular theism," Maxine replied.

I felt my lack of a hat. I would have liked something with a dense, draped veil, like Jackie wore to JFK's funeral, but that might have been a little too melodramatic, even for me. After all, Bridget and I had just been friends. So I wore the purple cashmere sweater that I'd bought to wear to dinner with Bridget. She noticed when I wore sensual fabrics.

Nancy, obviously pregnant, said she hoped her child would have the same adventurous spirit as Bridget. She quickly amended that to, "a little bit of Bridget's adventurous spirit."

Then Maxine stepped up to the podium, which had a vase of yellow, long-stemmed roses, sent by Robin, in front of it. "Bridget and I shared many things," she began.

Someone in the row behind me murmured, "Including girlfriends."

No mushrooms—not even canned ones—appeared among the funeral foods at Natalie's house. I appreciated her discretion.

I thought of all the community events and parties I'd been to with these same people. Bridget had always been there. Something hard hung in my chest, just below the hollow of my throat; hung like the unmoving pendulum of a clock stilled at the hour of Bridget's death. I moved through the room, listening for Bridget's voice, certain that at any minute she would emerge from Natalie's bedroom or kitchen.

"My ex's ex's ex is a nephrologist."

I recognized the speaker from a couple of Bridget's parties.

"That's disgusting," her companion said. "Light bondage is one thing, but dead people . . ."

"No, no—she's a kidney specialist."

"Oh! You called her when you heard about Bridget?"

"No, all of us had brunch together on Sunday. Anyway, she said that alcohol can be a contributing factor to the toxicity of certain mushrooms. Well, did you ever see Bridget drink less than a six-pack at a football party?"

Angel offered to bring me some food.

"I'm not really hungry," I said.

"I'm going to bring you something anyway."

A short time later she reappeared at my side with a plate of triangles of thin brown bread topped with smoked salmon and dill, and slices of pumpernickel layered with whole basil leaves, fresh mozzarella, and sun-dried tomatoes glistening with olive oil.

"Word is Maxine spent last night here, with Natalie," Angel said.

I shrugged. "Sometimes Natalie stayed with Bridget,

sometimes she stayed with Maxine. Some<s>tu</s>ines Bridget stayed with Natalie. Other times both Bridget and Maxine stayed with Natalie. And yet, as far as I know, Maxine never stayed with Bridget when Natalie wasn't there too."

"In other words," Angel said, "Nothing for anyone to get their boi shorts all bunched up about. Nothing that adds up to anything you would want to swear to in court."

Annalise wasn't satisfied with Natalie's approach to mourning. "This is foof," she declared. "Some of us are getting together tomorrow to play touch football. We're going to dedicate the game to Bridget. Be at our house by two o'clock."

"But I don't know how to play touch football."

Annalise's laughter rose in the rarefied air of Natalie's apartment like a flock of startled birds. People turned to look at her. "You're a femme, B.D.," she said. "Of course you don't know how to play touch football. I want you there because you loved Bridget."

After the game we wound up at a bar that Bridget had favored, but Natalie refused to set foot in. Strings of flamingo Christmas tree lights drooped over grimy windows, and paintings on velvet hung askew on the walls. I was drinking cosmopolitans; a pretty drink that packs a punch. Bridget was a bit like that.

Before long people were singing Broadway songs that reminded them of Bridget, or that they knew she had liked. Natalie and Maxine may not have approved of Bridget's penchant for bursting into song in public, but to me, it was one her most endearing qualities. I was preparing to do "I'm Just a Cock-eyed Optimist," from *South Pacific*, but when they handed the karaoke mike to me, I broke down and had to pass it on.

If I were lucky, Bridget would haunt me. I figured she'd make a swell, friendly ghost.

Chapter 26

"Natalie's invited me to go with her and Maxine to scatter Bridget's ashes," I told Angel. "They're doing it as part of a mushroom expedition." I didn't say that the combination of the two troubled my sense of propriety, despite Natalie's telling me this was one of the best times of the year to look for mushrooms. "I want to go because of what I feel for Bridget, but what do I know about mushrooms? I go to the supermarket and there they are in a blue plastic box with plastic wrap all around them, looking thoroughly sanitized, but of course I wash them anyway."

"Why do you have to know anything about mushrooms?"

"They might have poisoned Bridget. They could poison me." I paused to think about that for a minute. Natalie got to Bridget before I did here on earth, but up in heaven I could have first dibs. But then, Bridget had told me she wasn't going to heaven. "If I don't go, Natalie and Maxine might think I don't trust them."

"Do you trust them?"

"No, but I don't want them to know that I don't trust them."

"B.D., we've been over this," Angel said. "It was an accident; a horrible accident. There's no way it was deliberate. If you're going to poison someone with mushrooms, you don't put them on a pizza you're serving to a dozen people. Besides, what would their motive be?"

"With Bridget out of the way, they could be together," I said.

Angel sighed. "B.D., when someone is in a relationship and they want to be with someone else, they break up the relationship; they don't murder the person they no longer want to be with. Just imagine if we had dead bodies instead of exes."

So I ended up going—because I'd decided there was something I wanted to do: claim just a bit of Bridget's ashes for myself.

Natalie and Maxine had bought a cottage together about a month after Bridget died. The surrounding woods and abandoned apple orchards were excellent hunting grounds for mushrooms.

I'd pictured a rustic wooden cabin, quaintly furnished with flea market finds. But when I walked into the front room, I found built-in bookcases, plush oriental rugs and a fireplace lintel that looked like marble. I made a mental note to tell Eduardo about the Waterford crystal hurricane lamps.

"That opens out into a bed," Maxine said, gesturing toward a massive, brown leather sofa.

"Wait till you see the kitchen," Natalie said.

At one time, the kitchen probably had a white, enameled stove and sink and a refrigerator that knocked and hummed. But Natalie had banished them to appliance limbo. The sunlight streaming through the Andersen windows now reflected off stainless steel and Portuguese tile.

I followed Natalie into the bedroom, noting immediately that there was one queen-sized brass bed. But what did it matter anyway, now that Bridget was gone?

—*ɯɯ*—

Natalie had offered the urn with the ashes to Bridget's mother, but Mrs. McKnight declined. She was one of those people who need a place to leave flowers and a marker to look at, so she'd arranged for an empty grave with a headstone for Bridget in the family plot. I was glad. Remembering my visit to the McKnight house with Eduardo the day of Nancy's wedding, I didn't want what was left of Bridget to be surrounded by those porcelain figurines.

Natalie went outside with the urn alone. When she returned about a half hour later she gave me the urn. "Here, you can sprinkle the rest of her as we go along."

"Or, if you see a particular spot that you think Bridget might like, you can dump what's left all at once," Maxine said.

Natalie and Maxine were carrying baskets, small trowels, and pocketknives. Maxine had a roll of wax paper and a couple of field guides in a small knapsack.

Though the woods were a better location than a living room or den, I couldn't help feeling that the rim of a volcano would be the ideal drop-off spot for Bridget's ashes. But I wasn't going to be near a volcano anytime soon.

The trees were at their full fall glory—shades of yellow and red glinting in bright sunlight. Off to my left, a flock of black birds swirled up and over to another spot.

I had brought a small brass box that had belonged to my aunt Rose with me. While Natalie and Maxine were stooped over something, presumably a mushroom, I poured some of Bridget's ashes into the box, which I put back into my jacket pocket.

As I caught up with them, Maxine was reading one of her field guides. I heard Natalie say, "Really? Do you think that's what it is?"

We spent a couple of hours in the woods. I scattered all of Bridget's ashes except for the ones in the box in my pocket.

When we returned to the cottage, I watched Maxine remove the mushrooms from the basket. Natalie was doing something with a skillet.

"Since we didn't have any lunch," Maxine said, "we'll have some mushrooms with our tea."

"Because of Bridget's death, we know that we have to be really, really careful about eating any mushrooms we're not one-hundred-percent sure we can identify," she added.

"That one's blue," I said.

"It just got a little bruised in the basket," Maxine replied.

"I don't want to eat it if it's blue." I was trying really hard not to whine.

"I'll cut the blue parts off before I cook it," Natalie said.

I went into the living room and sat down on the brown leather sofa, wondering how I was going to get out of this. Soon Natalie came in from the kitchen with mushrooms on three small plates. Maxine followed her carrying a tray with a teapot, three mugs, spoons and honey.

I looked at the mushrooms. I looked at Maxine. I looked at Natalie.

"They got a little burnt, but they should taste fine," Natalie said.

Natalie was looking at me. Maxine was looking at me. The mushrooms might have been looking at me too, all of us awaiting our fates.

Maxine began eating. I watched her carefully for a couple of minutes. Then Natalie started in.

I put a forkful of mushrooms in my mouth, chewed carefully, and quickly swallowed them. "Very interesting."

"Tea?" Natalie asked.

Everything was fine until I noticed that the flames in the fireplace were forming fiery Rorschach patterns. Trying to decide what they represented made it hard to focus on what Natalie and Maxine were saying. I wondered if I might be dying. Was I breathing normally? Should I ask to go to the emergency room? If there even was one around here?

I guess I must have looked a little strange because Maxine went into her mom mode, which involved concentrated fussing and concerned cooing. I had seen her do this with other people, and being on the receiving end was as pleasurable an experience as I had imagined. I decided that I wasn't dying after all. What with the tea and being so close to the fire, I was very warm and a little dizzy so the two of them helped me out of my clothes and into the sofa bed. I kept trying to ask them to get my pajamas out of my backpack, but they probably couldn't understand what I was saying.

What happened next was almost certainly a dream. It's embarrassing to have to tell about it.

The moon was pressed up against the windowpane, smiling in at me with Bridget's face. Stars had fallen through the roof and into the room. Something smooth and cool was swirling over and around my body, and somehow my hands became tangled in it. Someone slipped a blindfold over my eyes, yet I continued to see.

Bridget was a graceful many-armed goddess, flicking a golden tongue in time with one that would dart across my right nipple from time to time. As my body arched toward that tongue, flower turning up to sun, another mouth closed over my left nipple and began a gentle sucking.

I was staring into Bridget's eyes, I was looking into the ocean, I was floating with my legs spread wide and the water lapped up against me and I heard gulls crying. Or maybe that was me?

"I had a really weird dream last night," I said, as I cut into the perfectly cooked herb and cheese omelet Natalie had set before me. "It was one of the most intensely sexual dreams I've ever had."

"Well, those kinds of dreams are the best," Maxine replied.

"I fell asleep right away," Natalie said. "We'd like to head back to the city after breakfast if that's okay with you, B.D. We've done everything we wanted to do here."

I told her that was fine with me.

Our return trip was quiet. Natalie played classical music on the car's CD player; none of us spoke very much. They dropped me off in front of my apartment building, and I never saw either one again.

Chapter 27

In preparation for a new year, I transferred the birthdays and anniversaries noted in my old date book into my new one. When I came to the square for April 1, I wrote in Bridget's name.

And if, in the privacy of my apartment, I sometimes said her name aloud, well, that was nobody's business but my own.

Bridget didn't haunt me in a scary, spectral way. Nor in a friendly, intimate way, like Captain Daniel Gregg in *The Ghost and Mrs. Muir*, which I would have welcomed. But there were times I thought I saw her, even though I knew it couldn't be.

In June, cruising the crowd going into Madison Square Garden for a New York Liberty basketball game, I became fixated on the nape of a woman's neck. The cut and color of her hair, the way she was standing with her hands in her pockets, made me silently beg, *turn around, turn around.* I knew it couldn't be Bridget, but I needed to see the face, feel the disappointment; feel like the fool that I was.

Today, I thought I saw Bridget again.

I remember her walk as being more of an amble than

the glide of the woman ahead of me. Bridget hated wearing socks, but even she would have to suffer for the sake of those flat, black loafers. As I moved closer, I saw that the shoes weren't shiny, but scuffed, as Bridget's surely would be.

Her pants were black and wide-legged, some soft fabric that billowed and swirled as she strode down the pavement. The gray tweed jacket was much too stylish—short, tucked at the waist, then flaring out. And those highlights in her hair came from time spent in a salon chair, something Bridget would have scorned. So why was I staring, thinking it might be her?

She turned around, hand supplementing the shade provided by her sunglasses. She could have been looking for someone, at someone—maybe even at me. I stared down at the pavement.

When I looked up again, she was gone; vanished like a mirage of water in the desert.

Maybe the two of us had some unfinished business when she died. Maybe Bridget really was the one, the only one, for me. Of course, that can never be put to the test. Death is the *ne plus ultra* of unavailability.

—◢◤◥◣—

I named a star for Bridget. The International Star Registry included two star-locating charts with the certificate they sent me, but I just look up at the sky, as I'm doing tonight.

They say to really see the stars you have to go to a place where there are no city lights to distract from or diminish their splendor. Still, tonight in New York City, the summer night is perfect. The air has cooled to a silken temperature, and caresses my skin. I want to float naked in this tranquil darkness, but all I can do is look up—beyond the dark towers stamped with rectangles of lamplight, to the star-studded sky.

It's tempting to think that the brightest star is Bridget's star, but I remember reading that the brightest stars are really planets.

One day—not too soon, but one day—I'll take a trip. I'll do it for my fiftieth birthday. I'll invite Angel, if we're still together. Maybe even if we're not. I'll ask Erica, my cousin Sarah, and Cathy to charter a boat with me—and we'll sail the Galapagos Islands. We'll look for blue- and red-footed boobies, flightless cormorants, lava herons, and giant tortoises. I'll make sure we're there at the right season, so we can watch Pacific green sea turtles mating. I've read that the turtles can roll in the water for hours in their copulatory embrace.

I'll bring along the little bit of Bridget's ashes that I've saved. You aren't supposed to leave anything like that on the islands, but I'll be able to scatter the ashes somewhere in Ecuador or at sea. And, in the still of the night, I'll lie on the deck of our little ship, stare up into the night sky full of shimmering stars, and remember her. Then, when I sleep, I'll dream of embracing Bridget, gently rolling for hours as two turtles together in the sea.

About the Author

Carol Rosenfeld is an accomplished short fiction writer and poet—though it's been a while since she participated in a poetry slam. *The One That Got Away* is the first novel by this writer described as "A fruit cup in the whole-grain world of literary fiction." A Juris Doctor (she studied at night school!), she is kept very busy as the voluntary chair of the Publishing Triangle, which has been promoting LGBT literature since 1988. And that's when she's not at her day job, working for an organization that administers grants for the many colleges in the City University of New York.

She's lived in New York since 1976, and can often be found at the opera—she has a growing fascination for Wagner (and quite a few questions, too).

At Bywater Books we love good books about lesbians just like you do, and we're committed to bringing the best of contemporary lesbian writing to our avid readers. Our editorial team is dedicated to finding and developing outstanding writers who create books you won't want to put down.

We sponsor the Bywater Prize for Fiction to help with this quest. Each prize winner receives $1,000 and publication of their novel. We have already discovered amazing writers like Jill Malone, Sally Bellerose, and Hilary Sloin through the Bywater Prize. Which exciting new writer will we find next?

For more information about Bywater Books and the annual Bywater Prize for Fiction, please visit our website.

www.bywaterbooks.com